A Paper Trail
Book 3 in the My Paper Heart Saga
Magan Vernon

For information visit www.maganvernon.com

Summary: Passing her first semester of community college? Done.

Getting her boyfriend an amazing birthday gift? Done.

Throwing up in New Orleans on said boyfriend's birthday? Yeah...about that...

Everything in Libby's life was falling into place...or she thought it was.

After a night of sin in New Orleans, she thought she might just be sick from exhaustion but a trip to the doctor proved otherwise.

Now instead of moving forward, her and commit-a-phobic boyfriend Blaine Crabtree have to go in a completely new direction.

Every road block has gotten in their way. Everything to tear them apart. Now they have to figure out if they are strong enough to move forward or if this is the end of their paper trail

First Edition, September 2015

Cover Design by Sharp Cover Designs

http://www.sharpcoverdesign.com/

Cover photography by Michael Meadows Studios

http://www.michaelmeadowsstudios.com/

Cover model: Brandon Lane

https://www.facebook.com/Brandonromance2846

Edited by Kellie Montgomery at Eye Candy Bookstore

http://www.eyecandybookstore.com/

Dedicate to you
Yes. YOU.
The one who took a chance.
The one who picked up this series and kept reading. Kept messaging me and telling me how much you loved these characters.
This is all for you.

Praise for The My Paper Heart Saga

[Vernon] is an eloquent writer and knows how to really develop her characters! I look forward to more of her work! - Heather at Nightly Reading Reviews

Her sassy female lead, Libby, puts the 'fun' in funny and makes *My Paper Heart* **an extremely entertaining read!-** *Candace at Lovey Dovey Books*

I really enjoyed this story of finding love and discovering who you truly are. - *Laura at Bookish Treasers on My Paper Heart*

I love Magan's honest style of writing. Her characters have flaws and make mistakes. And her love scenes are a mix of sexy and sometimes hilariously awkward!

- Amy at The Reading Realm on On Paper Wings

Chapter 1

I was sick. Not the "Oh-I-have-a-cold-and-can't-stop-my-sniffles-sick," but the all out, dry heaving in the toilet kind.

It didn't help that I was sick for my first Mardi Gras in Louisiana or that it was my boyfriend Blaine's birthday and he wanted to spend Fat Tuesday in New Orleans.

I stared at myself in the bathroom mirror; there was no amount of makeup that would cover my dark circles. I was trying to look as cute as possible, but my period had to be coming because I was also bloated and nothing was fitting right. I just wanted to stay home on the couch and watch reruns of reality TV.

But I knew that wasn't going to happen.

I adjusted the straps of my deep purple dress. I picked it out to pair with my gold booties and peacock headband for the occasion. I thought it was festive for my first Fat Tuesday parade, but now I was just feeling more fat than celebratory.

My nutritionist and therapist constantly told me that I had to stop with the "self-hate" behavior, but when I was moody and bloated, it was hard to do.

"Libby? Are you all right in there?" Aunt Dee yelled from the other side of the bathroom door.

I spit out the toothpaste into the sink. All the dry heaving was seriously giving me horrible breath. "Yeah. I'm fine."

I fluffed out my hair and pinched my cheeks, trying to get some color back into them. I was supposed to be at Blaine's twenty minutes ago, but it was taking longer and longer to get ready with being sick.

I opened the door of the bathroom to see Aunt Dee standing there, wringing her hands like she always did when she was nervous.

"Are you sure you're okay, honey?" She stared at me behind those Coke bottle glasses. When I first moved in with her, I thought she was so fiery and full of life for someone her age, but as the months passed, it seemed like she had just gotten older and more tired. She started asking me to do more around her store and spent more time at home. I just really prayed something wasn't wrong with her. I was closer to her than my own mother and I couldn't imagine anything happening.

I offered her a small smile. "I promise, I'm fine Aunt Dee."

"You know, if you don't feel up to going to New Orleans tonight, don't do it. Don't force Blaine to make you do anything you don't want to."

I laughed slightly. "Aunt Dee, I'm fine."

"But I do have to get going. Blaine not so subtly hinted that he wanted new fog lights for his truck and the tracking says the package should be at his house. I don't want him opening it before I get there. The guy has absolutely no patience." I patted her back.

Aunt Dee nodded slowly. "Well, if you really think you're feeling up to it..."

I smiled and gave her a quick hug. "I do, Aunt Dee. I may be late tonight, though, so don't wait up. Okay?"

"Okay. Be careful. Text me when you leave New Orleans."

"Aunt Dee. It's going to be late."

She shook her head. "I don't care. I just want to make sure that you're all right. There is a reason there are forty days of Lent after Mardi Gras. There's so much sin and debauchery that you don't even want to go near it again."

I laughed. "I'm sure that's what they had in mind."

WHEN I PULLED UP TO the house, Blaine was already on top of his truck with a set of tools. The sun was starting to set, so he had a spotlight on him and every single light on the front of the house. He wasn't wearing a shirt and his tanned torso was glistening in sweat and covered in stripes of oil. That didn't stop me from licking my lips and staring at his wicked V. I may have been with him for almost a year, but I always found my eyes drawing to that spot.

I turned off my engine and got out, putting my hand on my hip. "Seriously, Blaine? You couldn't wait a few more minutes for me to get here before you opened it?"

He looked down from his truck. No matter how many times I saw his wide smile and bright blue eyes, they still did me in. I had to keep my heart from stopping and my breath from catching in my throat. He was too pretty for his own good.

"I kept the box. I could always put the extra parts back in there if you want to see me open them again."

I rolled my eyes. "I should have known and just had them sent to Aunt Dee's."

He hopped down from the truck and sauntered over until he was right in front of me. He looped his arms around my waist and pulled me closer. "But then you wouldn't get the pleasure of watching me install them."

Normally I would have found this sexy, feeling him pressed against me with only the thin material of my dress between us, but something was off. There was a smell that permeated off of him. It was metallic. Like his tools were recently sharpened or something. Either way, when it hit my nose, I had to step back and swallow the bile that was gathering in my mouth.

He cocked an eyebrow. "Are you okay, baby?"

I shook my head and swallowed hard. "Yeah. I'm fine. You just may need a shower before we leave."

He laughed and put his hand to his chest. "You don't like my eau-de-sweat?"

I wrinkled my nose. "No. No, I don't."

"All right, baby, I guess I've spent enough time out here anyway. I'll take a quick shower then Mom wants us to eat with them before we leave." He gave me a quick peck on my cheek.

"Okay. Sounds good." I nodded, but he was already running toward the front porch.

I decided to follow him in. He usually didn't take too long in the shower, so I figured I'd be the good girlfriend and ask his mom if she needed any help in the kitchen.

Or I would have, if the smell didn't stop me first.

It wasn't that his dogs had been out in the mud, it was something about the Cajun spices. Usually my mouth watered for them and now they were making my stomach churn, but I had to swallow it back. Being a girl with an eating disorder meant that I got a lot of stares if I ever got sick, or even if I just took too long in the bathroom. I knew the moment I'd start anything, I'd probably get sent back to the hospital.

So I sucked it up, held my breath, and walked into the kitchen.

Vicki stood over the stove with a dog on each side of her, staring up and licking their lips as they waited for something to drop.

"Blue, quit that!" She swatted the dog on the right with her free hand.

"Hey Vicki, anything I can help with?" I took a few more steps into the kitchen and tried to ignore the gurgling in my stomach.

Vicki smiled once she saw me and pushed her bright blonde hair over her shoulder. "I would, honey, but a Cajun woman's roux has to be her own."

I had no idea what she was talking about, so I just smiled.

Vicki pointed to a brightly colored circular pastry thing on the counter. "You can bring that out and put on the table if you want. Blaine loves his King Cake. And go say hi to Meemaw. She's in there with Alicia and Callie."

"Oh, sure." I picked up the King Cake and stared at the blobs of yellow, green, and purple frosting.

"Having a Mardi Gras baby works out well for these occasions," she said, stirring the big pot on the stove.

"It sure does," I said, not really sure if I agreed with that or not.

I carried the cake into the dining room and, just like Vicki had said, there was Blaine's grandma sitting at the head of the table with her ever present oxygen tank at her side. At least she didn't have a cigarette in her hand as she held Blaine's sister Alicia's one month old baby in her arms.

"Now be careful of her head, Meemaw," Alicia said, hovering over her.

Meemaw cradled the baby in her arms, staring down at the little girl with a hint of a smile. "Oh pish, Alicia, I've been taking care of babies since before you were even shitting in your britches. I know what I'm doing."

Alicia pushed her hair behind her ears. She had gotten it chopped off at some point during her pregnancy and with the short hair it made her hollow cheek bones and the circles under her eyes more prevalent. I don't know how the hell she did it with two young kids at home all day.

"Hi, guys," I said, setting the cake down on the table.

Meemaw looked up at me with a half-scowl. "Still a Yankee, I see?"

"Um, yes?" I said, not sure how else to answer.

"Pay her no mind, Libby," Alicia said and came over, giving me a big hug. I always liked Alicia; it was Meg, Blaine's oldest sister, that could put the fear of God into any girl.

"Before long, she'll be a Southerner, just you wait. Then Blaine will be pouring arsenic in my coffee so he can get my house," Meemaw said, still staring down at the baby, barely missing a beat.

I just stared at her and Alicia laughed to break the tension, so I followed suit. I knew Blaine was inheriting her house, but the way she was so nonchalant about it was always off-putting.

"Blaine! How long are you going to be up there? It shouldn't take you that long to scrub yourself unless you've been rolling in the mud!" Vicki yelled up the stairs.

"Be down in a sec, Ma!" Blaine yelled.

"So, how's school going?" Alicia asked, probably because she didn't have much else to talk about. We never really bonded. I hadn't with either of Blaine's sisters. Of course, we didn't have much in common. They were country girls who took care of their kids and I was the girl from Chicago...who was sleeping with their brother.

"Good. I have five classes this semester plus work, so I'm pretty busy."

"I imagine," Alicia said, smacking her lips.

Now I had to think of something else to make small talk about. "So, how are things with Callie? She's precious."

Alicia sighed. "Good. Busy. Very busy."

Thank God Blaine bolted down the stairs, putting his arm around my waist and kissing my forehead. He definitely smelled better when he was fresh out of the shower, and there was something about his wet hair that made him look even more kissable. Just not when his family was right there. "Do I smell better now?"

"You know, you can bathe a dog, but they still smell like wet dog," Alicia said, smacking Blaine in the stomach.

"Aw, you're too good to me, sis," Blaine said with a laugh.

Just then Blaine's niece, Abby, burst through the door in her ever-present tutu. "Happy Birthday Uncle Blaine! We got you tools!"

Blaine laughed and picked up the little girl in his arms as her mom, Meg, came in carrying her youngest daughter Ashley, with her husband Ronnie and their son Braiden following behind.

"Dangit, Abby, you ain't supposed to tell him what we got him!" Meg said, giving Blaine a side hug as he put down Ashley.

"It could be worse, you could have told me you got me something like bow ties," Blaine said.

Meg shook her head and winked at me. "Naw, I'll leave it to your lady to get you some of that frou frou Southern boy shit."

Blaine put his arm back around me. "Actually, Libby got me new fog lights on the truck, which means Ronnie and I need to go muddin.'"

"Hell yeah we do," Ronnie said, turning his camo hat around and giving Blaine a fist bump.

It was always a full house at the Crabtree's and the craziness was always a nice distraction. All the kids ran around until Vicki finally called them all in for prayers and supper. I wanted to eat every bit of the food and normally I would, but I found myself putting a bite to my lips and putting it back.

"Ma, can we just get to the cake now? Jackson and Dina are waiting on us, and we have to get to Don's," Blaine whined which deepened his Southern drawl.

His dad smacked the back of his head. "Just because it's your birthday, doesn't mean you can talk to your mom like that."

Blaine rubbed the back of his head. "Sorry, Ma."

Vicki smiled and stood up, grabbing a knife before cutting out a big piece of the cake and plopping it onto a paper plate and setting it in front of Blaine. "Only because I still have a sweet spot for my Mardi Gras baby."

"Abby wants cake too!" Blaine's niece, Abby, whined, followed shortly by the other nieces and nephews.

"Okay, okay. Just hold your horses," Vicki said and cut another piece and pushed a plate in front of me.

"Oh, no I'm fine without cake," I said, trying to wave it away.

Though Vicki always had great food, the few bites of Jambalaya and cornbread I had were already turning in my stomach.

"Nonsense, there is always room for cake," Vicki said, pushing the plate toward me.

I could feel the heat of everyone's eyes on me. Last time we were all together, I ran out of the room and passed out. That was before I ended up in the hospital. Now I felt like they were judging my every bite.

"Okay...I guess I can make room," I said and took the plate, holding up my fork and going in for a bite.

I put the piece in my mouth and bit down on something hard. "OW!"

I grabbed a napkin and tried to demurely spit whatever I bit into out, but it came out in a big wad. It was unlady-like but I had to see what it was and staring back at me was a little plastic baby.

"What the—?"

"LIBBY HAD A BABY!" Abby yelled.

Blaine looked over my shoulder. "Aw, Damn. I wanted the baby."

"I'm sure you'd technically be the father," Meg said.

"Uh...what?" I asked, staring between the two of them.

Blaine smiled and shook his head. "A plastic baby is put in every king cake. Whoever gets it is the Mardi Gras queen or king."

"Oh. Well, I guess that makes me the queen."

Blaine leaned in and kissed my cheek. "Always."

"Ewwwwww, gross," all the kids said and made gagging noises.

"You two better cut that out until you're married and have a real baby," Abby said.

Blaine just shook his head and sat back in his seat but gave me a quick wink.

If a kiss on the cheek was going to get that reaction, I was in for a hell of a show with the Mardi Gras parade.

Chapter 2

By the time we finally got around to leave, I was more than ready to get out of the house. Not just because my stomach was turning, but I was ready to be rid of the questioning stares from Meemaw.

Dina crawled into the backseat of the truck followed by Jackson. "Damn, Libby, think you're going to be able to drive this thing home when Blaine's too hammered to drive?"

"I never said I was getting wasted," Blaine said as he pulled out of the driveway.

"Sure you aren't. I'm sure Don won't have a cooler full with your name on it," Jackson added.

"I already told him I could drive if needed to," I said. I kind of knew that was going to be the case, which is why I suggested taking my car, but everyone refused to ride in the tiny back seat of my convertible.

"And if I need you to, then I'm sure you'll take good care of my truck." Blaine leaned in and gently kissed my lips.

"Enough with the PDA, get driving so we can get our drink on," Jackson yelled, patting the back of my head rest.

It was usually only about a forty-five minute drive to New Orleans, but with detours for the parade route and just about every tourist making their way into the city, we were going on almost two hours before we finally rolled in front of Don's duplex.

We were barely out of the car when Don came barreling out, wearing a way-too-revealing gold man thong and a purple mask. "HAPPY MARDI GRAS!"

He downed a big plastic glass of something red and then hopped on Blaine's back.

"Well, someone's already started the party," Dina said.

"Yeah and y'all better catch up," Don said, hopping off of Blaine and then grabbing drinks from the cooler next to him.

I shook my head. "I'm not drinking. DD."

He laughed. "You're such a good girlfriend, Libby. If I was into blonde Yankees, I'd take you home to meet my mama."

"Yeah and if you didn't prefer dudes," Jackson said, smacking Don on the ass with his free hand.

"You're just jealous," Don said, practically skipping to his front door.

We followed Don into the duplex, where it looked like Mardi Gras threw up. It was a small, front room with a dark wooden floor and a few couches, but every bit of furniture had a half-dressed person on it and all the other surfaces were covered in beads or various bottles and cups.

Don pointed to the people sitting around and introduced them quickly, but half his words were slurred and the other half were him laughing.

"Let me get y'all a drink that isn't whatever shit beer Don pulled out of the cooler," a girl said. She had very tanned skin and wore a dress that looked like it was made of green, purple, and gold beads.

I waved my hands in front of my face. "I'm good. I'm not drinking. I'm driving."

She laughed. "Well we ain't going anywhere, honey. The Quarter is for the tourists who get drunk and gropey. The Garden District is where it's at."

"Oh, I didn't know we were staying here." I looked around the room. Not that there was anything wrong with staying around there, I just expected my first Mardi Gras to be on Bourbon Street. Though the way my stomach was acting and the fact that I was exhausted, it was probably better just to stay chill.

The girl smiled. "Well, that's more like it. How about I make you a Hurricane? I make the best in three parishes."

I nodded. "I guess. I can share it with Dina if I need to"

I turned to see if Dina had my back but she and Jackson were already engaged in a conversation with another couple.

I went to look back at the girl but she was already in the kitchen, pouring random bottles of liquor into the blender.

Shit. What had I gotten myself into?

I'D NEVER ACTUALLY gotten the drink or anything, for that matter. Some commotion had started outside and everyone ran past me with their drinks in their hands.

I didn't know what I expected from a Mardi Gras parade but what I got was a lot of beads, boobs, and beer.

Every single person crowded on the tiny front lawn and waved their arms in the air, while spilling their drinks, just to maybe get something thrown from one of the floats.

If I wasn't sober, maybe I would have been as excited for some plastic beads.

Or if I wasn't exhausted.

Seriously, I didn't even have class that day and I was already dead on my feet. Maybe it was just the sickness taking hold, or maybe I really had been working too hard.

Now that I was officially a sophomore, I wanted to be able to finish community college within a year. That meant I loaded up classes on Tuesday and Thursday and worked Monday, Wednesday, and Friday. I was already signed up for a full schedule of summer classes as well. I wish I didn't slack off so much when I failed out of Illinois State, but I guess everything happens for a reason. I wouldn't be in Louisiana if I didn't. Or watching my boyfriend take his shirt off and throw it at some wide-eyed girl just so she'd throw him a giant set of pink beads.

I sat back in one of the rockers on the front porch. There may have been a lot of activity going on, but I could feel my eyes fluttering with each rock.

"Shit, is she sleeping?" I heard someone whisper.

"Damn, is she that drunk?" Another person asked.

"Naw. She's just tired. She's had a lot of shit going on." Blaine's voice was one I definitely recognized, no matter if it was half-cocked.

"Well, you'd better wake her ass up if you want to head to Rue."

I wiped my eyes before slowly opening them. "I'm awake, assholes, so you can stop talking about me."

Blaine was standing in front of me with a wide grin on his face and his shirt still off, his body glistening with sweat as if he'd just come back from work or the gym. I used to think it was gross when a guy sweat, but the way it looked on Blaine's tanned skin was more lickable than anything else.

"Show her my work, bro," Don said, coming out of nowhere and slapping Blaine on the back.

Blaine laughed. "Oh, yeah, check it, Lib."

He turned around and revealed a pen drawing of a fleur de lis between his shoulder blades.

"Um, that's cool and pretty impressive that Don could draw a straight line in his state," I said.

Blaine laughed again before turning around. "Yeah. The guy could do any kind of art work blindfolded. But I'm going to trust an actual artist to do the real thing."

"Okay...I guess?"

Blaine put his hand out and I took it, letting him lift me out of the rocking chair. "So let's go."

"Go, where?"

"We're heading to Rue."

"And that is?" I cocked an eyebrow.

"Are you sure she isn't drunk?" Don laughed.

Blaine ignored him and took a step closer. "Baby, we're going to the tattoo parlor. I've wanted to get some more ink for a while and this seems like a good time to do it."

"Are you sure you want to do that right now?" I asked.

Blaine smiled. "Sometimes you just have to live in the moment, baby."

IT WAS A WAY FARTHER walk than I thought it would be to the tattoo parlor. Probably because the streets were packed with people and the more upscale area of the Garden District wasn't exactly packed with tattoo parlors.

At least Don had put on some pants, but both boys still weren't wearing shirts. I guess they figured they could get away with it since barely anyone was clothed on the streets.

The Rue was along a street of brightly colored houses. It was electric yellow with a big, flashing neon "Open" sign in the window. Walking in, it was like Mardi Gras never stopped with the loud music, colorful chairs, and artwork covering all of the paneled walls.

"You sure you want to do this?" I asked Blaine for about the hundredth time.

He squeezed my hand. "Of course I am, baby. Why? Do you not want me to get this done?"

I stared at the walls of art work. There were rows and rows of paper with ink drawings of tribal symbols or other things that I'd seen on just about every sorority girl and fraternity boy on campus. It wasn't something I ever thought about doing myself, but definitely something I could see that people liked to show their individuality. As long as it wasn't a Chinese symbol that probably didn't mean what that person thought it did.

"All right, Crabtree, you ready?" a Cajun woman's voice bellowed.

I turned toward the voice and saw a large black woman with two full sleeves of tattoos and a shirt that read "Pain is inevitable. Suffering is optional."

Blaine nodded. "Yeah. I'm ready."

She waved him back and shuffled toward a black leather chair. I followed behind them slowly, wondering if it was typical for a woman that looked more like a voodoo priestess with her long black dreads and burning incense, to be a tattoo artist.

"Okay, Crabtree, what are you in for?" the woman asked, sitting down on a wheeled stool.

Blaine turned his back to her and waved his hand as far as he could up his back."I want this. Right here."

She laughed. "Well, if you want me to just take a Sharpie over it, I can."

"Naw. My buddy Don did this and I like it enough to make it permanent," Blaine said, pointing his thumb in Don's direction.

Don stood in the corner, just grinning.

The woman raised an eyebrow. "Are you sure? You know this thing is going to be permanent on your body forever."

Blaine nodded at the woman's arms. "Were you sure about yours?"

She laughed. "Some of them. Some I just got because I was a dumb kid and Louisiana lets you get tattoos at any age as long as you have parental consent."

"One of the things I love about Louisiana. There are rules, but it lets you have your own individuality. I've lived here all my life in St. Bernard parish and I don't plan on ever leaving. It's where my heart is and I want to know that if I've got Louisiana's back, it always has mine," Blaine said.

The woman nodded and a broad smile appeared on her face. "Okay, Mr. Crabtree. You convinced me. Now lay down, so we can make that ink more permanent."

I was fine watching Blaine lay face down on the chair while watching the lady prep him. I was fine when she started tracing and getting the ink ready.

But once the hum of the needle started and hit his skin, a trickle of blood leaked out. Then I was done.

My stomach lurched and my eyelids fluttered. "Um. I'm going to use the bathroom," I managed to squeak out.

"Down the hall and to the right by the back door, honey," the tattoo artist said, not taking her eyes off of her work.

"Thanks," I muttered, before I quickly turned around and rushed in the other direction.

I opened the black door that was at the end of the hall and prayed that it actually was the bathroom. I sighed a breath of relief when I turned on the light in the little red room and saw the toilet.

Slowly, I closed the door behind me and stared in the mirror above the pedestal sink.

It was the first time I looked at my reflection in a while and it wasn't a pretty sight.

I turned on the water and rinsed off my face, but dark circles and pale skin aren't easily washed away.

I kept scrubbing, even though I knew I had make up on, but the makeup wasn't covering anything, in fact, I think it made me look worse.

I barely heard the knock on the door and only knew there was a knock because it slowly opened and Blaine stood there, looking at my reflection. "Are you okay, baby?"

I met his eyes in the mirror. His face was crimson and his shirt was still off. I may have looked and felt like shit, but, damn, did he look good standing there in nothing but his jeans. Since it was springtime, he'd been working longer hours and all that time working with his hands had made his arms more developed. I loved tracing each line of his hard bicep.

"Yeah. Sorry. I guess I'm kind of a wimp."

He stepped behind me and put his hands on my shoulders; his warm finger tips trailed down the length of my arms before he leaned in and brushed his lips against my shoulder. "You're fine, baby. More than fine. You've been great. Not many other girls would do everything you've done for me, even when you feel like shit."

I smiled. "It's your birthday, and our first one together, I wasn't going to miss it."

He moved the strap of my dress to the side and his lips lingered just above my skin before he kissed my shoulder, then moved his mouth to my neck, causing goose bumps to form everywhere his lips grazed. "One of the many reasons why you're the best," he whispered.

An involuntary moan escaped my lips as his finger tip-toed down to my thighs. His hands splayed against my warm flesh while his thumbs inched up the hemline of my dress. Delicately slow, his thumbs slid under my dress and ran along the silk of my underwear.

"Do you think this is the place to be doing that, especially when you have a new tattoo?" I asked, but knew the moment his fingers slipped beneath my panties that I didn't exactly care where we were.

"Doing what exactly?" he whispered before nipping at my ear.

I opened my mouth to speak but instead only a whimper came out when he ran his thumb along my center.

"Hmmm..." He raised an eyebrow, his eyes locked on mine in the mirror. Blaine slid one finger inside of me while his thumb circled my sensitive flesh.

I had to bite down hard on my bottom lip to keep from moaning as I pushed myself against his hand, burying his fingers deeper. My whole body perked up from his touch and I felt more alive than I had all day. All it took was one hook of his finger and I was coming hard on him and couldn't hold in the little gasp that escaped my lips.

"Damn, baby, you're so wet," Blaine whispered into my shoulder.

I arched my back and moaned again as he twirled his fingers inside of me. He put one hand on my waist and then slowly pulled his hand back. I whimpered, already missing the feel of him. But he quickly spun me around so that I was facing him.

With his free hand, he pulled me toward him and I melted into him as his mouth met mine, his tongue dancing behind my lips as if he were savoring all of me.

I groaned, sliding my panties off, wanting to be closer. Wanting him to take me. Yes we were in the bathroom of a tattoo parlor, but there was something about his bare chest, the way his hands roamed, and I found myself panting with need.

"Think anyone is going to notice you're gone?" I asked, undoing his belt.

He grinned and pulled his wallet out of his back pocket. "N—"

Before he could finish his word, a knock came at the door. "Hey, you two aren't knocking boots in there, are you?"

"Shit," Blaine muttered.

I picked my underwear off the ground and shoved them in my purse. "Guess we'll have to continue this later," I whispered.

Blaine cocked an eyebrow and looked at my purse, then to me. "If you're not going to wear those, then that's all I'm going to be thinking about."

I shot him a wink before opening the door to a wide-eyed Don. Then I looked back at Blaine. "Think all you want."

Chapter 3

"**A**re you sure y'all don't want to just stay here?" Don asked. He stood in the doorway, the party still going on in full swing behind him.

Jackson laughed. "And where in the hell are we supposed to sleep? On the floor with twenty of your cousins?"

Don shook his head. "Hey, this is the south. We're used to it."

Blaine put his arm around me. "Even so, I think we're going to have to pass. If Libby has trouble staying awake on the ride home, I'll try and help her out."

"By helping her out, I hope you don't mean you plan on finger banging her while we're in the backseat," Jackson said, raising an eyebrow.

Blaine grinned. "Naw, I'll wait until we drop y'all off and do it on the hood of the truck in your driveway."

Jackson frowned. "You'd better be kidding Crabtree."

Blaine just laughed and somehow I had the feeling that he wasn't joking, but if he thought I was climbing onto the hood of his truck in the middle of the night when there were bugs out, then he was in for a rude awakening.

WE DROPPED JACKSON and Dina off at their place. After Christmas, they had moved in together. One of Dina and I's co-workers said it was way too soon for them to be moving in when they just got back together, but I didn't comment. Truth be told, I was hoping at some point Blaine would suggest moving in together as well.

Not that I didn't love living with Aunt Dee, but it would be nice to not have to worry about her walking in on us if we were trying to fool around, or to have a curfew at twenty years old.

"So...about what we started at the tattoo parlor." Blaine's hand slid up my leg, resting right where the hem of my skirt met my bare skin.

"Careful. You don't want to distract me and have me go off the side of the road in your truck."

I looked at him out of the corner of my eye and he was grinning. "I'd take the hit on my insurance. It'd be worth it."

"Gee, how romantic. You'd let me wreck your car so you can finger me." I rolled my eyes.

"Hey, I wouldn't say it that way. I can do things all romantical and shit."

I snorted. "Romantical and shit? That's even better."

"Fine, turn off on Conger road instead of going toward my house." He pointed out the window.

"No! I'm not going to pull over and have sex with you! Do you remember what happened last time we did that? There was a cop banging on our window and I got my hair caught in your belt buckle."

He laughed and shook his head. "I'm not making you pull over for that, baby. Just give me a chance, will ya?"

I thought on it for a moment, but decided to get him the benefit of the doubt and turned onto Conger Rd.

"How far am I supposed to drive?" I asked, glancing at Blaine.

"Not much longer and you'll turn," he said, smiling like he had a secret.

It felt like I was driving forever and I was starting to think it was just a rouse to get me to stop and give in to him.

"Okay, you're going to see a big barn up here and you'll turn on the dirt road right before it," he said, pointing out the front window.

A gray barn that looked like it had more wooden planks on the ground than on the actual structure came into view.

"This one?" I asked.

"Yep that's the one."

I raised an eyebrow as I turned down the narrow dirt road. "This seems like something that would be in the beginning of a horror movie. They turned down the old dirt road and a guy with a chainsaw came out of the woods."

"I'm trying to do something nice and you go off talking about chainsaws."

"Doesn't it turn you on when I talk about power tools?" I raised an eyebrow.

He shook his head. "Baby, you're lucky you make me laugh."

"And why am I lucky? Would you not keep me around if I didn't?"

"No, then you'd just miss out on this." He pointed out the front window.

I looked at where his finger landed and could barely make out a sign. As I pulled the car closer, the silhouette of a 1950's car hop on a small billboard had the faded words "Elsbury Drive-In" scrawled across it.

"Don't you think it's a little late for a movie?" I asked.

Blaine shook his head. "This place has been shut down since the 1980's. At one point, they were going to bulldoze it and put in a Piggly Wiggly, but the funding fell through."

"So, why are we here now if there isn't a theatre?"

He smiled and nodded out the window. "Star gazing."

I cocked an eyebrow. "Really?"

"Yes, really. Just pull forward and you'll see."

I fumbled around the gear shift. "Where are your brights? I don't want to get lost or run into a man with a chainsaw."

Blaine put his hand on mine. "Baby, you're fine. Just trust me, okay?"

I met his eyes. Starring into his deep baby blues, there was no way I could ever say no to anything he asked.

"I do. Always."

He smiled and I looked back out the window, and slowly crept forward over a small hill. Once we were at the bottom of it, I gasped at the sight before me.

There were rows and rows of rusting white stands that probably once houses radios to listen to the movie, but now were empty. They all stood there like soldiers facing a large, white screen that was ripped down the middle. But that wasn't the impressive part.

Over the entire area was a large stretch of clear blue sky and millions of twinkly stars. It looked like something out of a planetarium that was manmade. There was nothing to obstruct the view, just the sky and the land before.

"Wow. This is really pretty."

Blaine laughed. "I told you."

I pulled and parked near one of the stands, wondering what I was supposed to do next. But Blaine decided that for me and reached over, turning off the car and putting the keys in his pocket.

"What are your plans now?" I asked, cocking an eyebrow.

He smiled and reached into the backseat, grabbing an LSU blanket before opening his door and hopping out.

"I told you no outdoor sex!" I yelled, getting out of the car and following him to the truck bed.

He shook his head. "I didn't say anything about that."

With that, he lowered the tailgate and hopped in the back of the truck, spreading out the blanket. He then reached his hand out to me. "Come here."

I raised a quizzical eyebrow, but gave him my hand anyway and let him help me into the truck. I took the seat next to him, waiting on his next move.

"Now lay down with me," he said.

I was going to protest, but he put his arm around me and pulled me at his side as he lay on his back.

If I thought the view was a sight coming into the theatre, it was even more beautiful lying down and looking at the sky above. Everything swirled in a mix of dark blue and purples with sprinklings of bright stars. The moon was a tiny crescent, like it was just an accessory to all of the constellations.

"How could someone pay attention a movie when they have this beautiful of a view over their heads?" I asked.

"I don't know. I haven't been able to pay attention to much else since the most beautiful girl walked into my life. Even the stars."

I smiled and looked over at Blaine. "That was really cheesy."

He leaned over and brushed a fallen curl behind my ear. "But true."

I stared at the blue of his eyes. Even in the dark, they were brighter than the night sky. I could get lost in his stare all day every day and probably wouldn't pay attention to a movie on the screen if it were right in front of us. Not when I had him there.

As if Blaine knew exactly what I was thinking, he leaned forward and lightly kissed my lips. It wasn't frantic and lustful like in the tattoo shop, but sweet and longing.

He cupped my face and deepened the kiss, his tongue teasing my bottom lip before it met mine with a little gasp escaping my mouth. I trailed my hands to his back, feeling the muscles through his thin t-shirt. With that, he pulled me closer, my body flush with his as goose bumps pricked every bit of skin that wasn't touching him.

Blaine broke the kiss slightly, his fingers trailing down my arm. "Are you cold, baby? You're shaking."

I shook my head, biting down on my lip. "No, but I wouldn't object to you warming me up."

He grinned, his fingers moving down my arm until they stopped at my waist, running against the fabric of my dress as if he was asking for my permission before he continued.

I pressed against him, feeling his bulge press against my core. I may have said I wouldn't do anything outdoors, but there was something about being under the stars that had be rethinking everything.

While Blaine's hands moved farther down, his lips also traced my neck. "Remember the first time you said you loved me and it was under the stars? We were lying on that blanket at my parents' and you tried to pretend like you didn't."

Way to be a buzzkill. My body stiffened."Yeah. You didn't even respond."

He moved his head up and his eyes met mine. "I think part of me was scared shitless and the other part of me was shocked. I wasn't expecting it and at the same time I was thinking, *damn, why didn't I say it first?* Or at all? This girl is pouring herself out to me and I just keep running like a damn fool."

"We don't need to talk about this now," I pressed, growing more and more uncomfortable with each word.

He shook his head. "No, we do. I may be a little buzzed and really fucking horny, but I also need you to know that I love you. I should have said it the first time months ago, and I will keep saying it every damn day. I love you more than every single star in the Louisiana sky above us."

"I love you too, Blaine. I always will," I whispered, before sealing my words with a kiss and rolling over so that I was on top of him.

He laughed. "I thought you were the one who didn't want to do anything but look at the stars?"

I sat up and slowly peeled off my dress with a small smile on my lips. "I didn't know how good the view was from up here."

He grinned and traced the curve of my breast. "It sure is. Especially when you don't wear a bra or panties."

"No need to. And it makes for easier access," I whispered and leaned forward, brushing my lips against his and my chest to his. His hands gripped my waist and he pulled me closer and I rocked my hips against his, causing a groan to escape his mouth.

His fingers trailed down the length of my butt, until he clasped it with his hands, his nails digging into me before his thumb traced my center.

"You're still so wet, baby," he murmured as I trembled.

I leaned back and pulled his shirt over his head. He had borrowed one from Don and I almost wished he didn't, it hid his amazing bronzed body that looked like it was carved by a sculptor. I trailed my fingers down the contours of his abs, then clawed to get his belt buckle undone as fast as I could. I wanted him as close as possible and as soon as possible. He shucked his pants off, leaving only the thin fabric of his underwear between us.

I moaned, grinding my core into his bulge and feeling how ready he was for me. He reached into his pants pocket and pulled out his wallet, quickly grabbing a condom and releasing his massive erection from his boxers.

"Here, let me do that. It is your birthday after all." I smiled and grabbed the condom, ripping it open with my teeth before sliding it on him.

His eyes barely shut as he leaned back and I pulled the rest of his boxers off. Slowly, I mounted him, letting every inch of him fill me up to the hilt. I let out a deep breath and rocked forward as he grasped onto my hips, moving our bodies to the same rhythm.

He circled his hips, causing every bit of him to hit the right spots and I cried out over and over, not sure how much exquisite pleasure I could take. Every movement kept making me come harder and harder.

"Damn, baby, you're not going to make me last long," he murmured, gritting his teeth and gripping my ass.

"I want you to come for me," I said, pushing forward and moving his hand to my core where his thumb found my sweet spot, circling it and making me cry out. I threw my head back, feeling my entire body shudder, followed by his.

I collapsed onto his chest and lay there, breathing in sync to the rhythm of his heart. For a while we just stayed there, still connected and staring up at the stars.

"Happy birthday, Blaine," I whispered.

He laughed, breathing through his nose and onto my hair. "Yeah. It definitely is."

Chapter 4

I had no idea what time I came back home. I knew the sun hadn't yet risen and after tangling naked with Blaine for far too long in the back of his truck, I was more than exhausted.

That and I was still sick. Like the never ending wave of nausea that liked to wake me out of a dead sleep.

A knock came at the door. I thought I was home alone. Granted, I didn't exactly know what time it was, but I figured Aunt Dee would be at work and Britt at school.

"Libby?" Aunt Dee's sweet Southern accent wafted through the door.

"Yeah?" I asked, trying to clear my throat.

"I made an appointment at the Elsbury clinic this morning for you at ten."

I opened the door, staring at my aunt. "You what?"

She wrung her hands together and looked everywhere but at me. "Well, I thought it might have been, you know, from too much partying, but you've been sick every day this week now. You look terrible, everyone at work agrees."

"Gee, you really know how to make a girl feel good about herself."

Aunt Dee sighed. "You know what I mean. Please just go for me? Maybe they'll just say it's some virus and you need to stay in bed and have soup all day, but it would make me feel better if you went."

I smiled. No matter what, I couldn't resist Aunt Dee's caring personality. "Okay. For you, I'll go."

THE ELSBURY CLINIC was just off the main downtown area. There were many times that Aunt Dee walked there from her shop when she needed to pick up a prescription or one of the doctors wanted her to bring in something they saw in the shop window.

The building was a newer one with a brick facade and the inside looked sterile with blue chairs, blue carpet, and white walls like every other doctor's office I'd ever been in.

I approached the counter, where a younger looking woman in blue scrubs sat. She opened a glass window and beamed at me as if seeing me was the highlight of her day.

"Hi, how can I help you?" she asked, her accent so thick you couldn't slice it with a butter knife.

"Hi. I'm Elizabeth, Libby, Gentry. I have an appointment at ten."

She turned and started typing into the large computer next to her. "Okay, I see that we have you in with Dr. Gene. Have a seat and we'll call you when she's ready for you."

"Okay, thank you." I nodded and took a seat in one of the uncomfortable blue waiting room chairs. There were a few magazines on a table in front of me so I thumbed through them. Most were maternity ones and the others were at least a few months old. I had no interest in being a mother or reading about a celebrity scandal from November, so I settled for scrolling Facebook on my phone.

By the time my name was called, I'd gone through half my friend's list and was more than ready to go back. I followed a short, stout woman in blue scrubs down a short hallway where she got my height and weight. I thought we were going to go into a room, but instead she held out a small plastic cup. "The doctor wants a urine sample from you."

I stared at the cup and raised an eyebrow. "Um, why?"

"Are you sexually active?" she asked bluntly.

"Um...that's not something you should ask when you first meet someone."

She smirked. "But it is something you ask at a doctor's office and with your symptoms the doctor just wants to check."

I sighed and took the cup from her. "Okay. There's no way I could be pregnant, but I'll do it."

Her smirk turned into a slight smile. "The bathroom is right around the corner to the left. There will be a little door near the sink, please open it and place the specimen there. When you're done, you can wait for the doctor in room two."

I nodded. "Okay. Thanks."

I couldn't remember the last time I had to pee in a cup and suddenly got pee shy. But after a few minutes, and playing some water sounds on my phone, I finally squeezed out a little bit and put it on the window marked "for urine samples". After that, I walked into room two.

After sitting in there for another few minutes, I thought the doctor would be in, but instead the same nurse came back in. "Sorry, were you expecting someone else?" she asked.

"Uh, yeah. Sorry, it's been a while so I thought the doctor was coming in."

She smiled again. "Sorry, I just have to ask you some more questions and get your vitals and some blood before you see her. Don't worry, it won't be long."

After some more questions, that I already answered when I filled out my health history form, blood pressure taken, and a few vials of blood, the nurse left again, saying the doctor would be in soon.

By soon I thought a few minutes, but as the minutes ticked down, I found my eyelids growing heavily and I was fast asleep when the door opened again and my eyes snapped open.

An older Cajun woman with a tight black bun and a white lab coat came into the room. "Sorry if I woke you, Ms. Gentry."

"Oh, no. I wasn't asleep," I said, but my own body failed me and I yawned.

The doctor nodded and took the wheeled stool across from me. "Now, let's just go over your symptoms here again, shall we?" She opened the manila folder on her lap.

It took everything I had to hold back an eye roll.

"You have had nausea, trouble sleeping at night and always tired during the day, swelling, and anything else I'm missing?" she asked.

"That sounds about right. Sounds like the flu to me and a round of antibiotics," I replied, hoping to just get out of there. I hated going over the same details over and over.

"And, Ms. Gentry, can you tell me the start of your last period?"

I chewed on my bottom lip. "Well, you see, I've kind of had a nutritional problem that I've been seeing a doctor for and my period comes and goes, so I couldn't really say."

That was a nice way to put it. I had bulimia and there would be months I'd go without my period, but I didn't want to go into that.

"And you're sexually active, I presume?" she asked, raising her eyebrows.

"Um, yes." I could feel the heat rise in my cheeks.

She scanned through the manila folder. "So, it shouldn't come as a shock that when we ran your urine sample, it tested positive for pregnancy?"

My mouth went completely dry and my eyes felt like they were about to bug out of my head. "What did you just say?"

She closed her folder and folded her hands on top of it. "Ms. Gentry, your symptoms were right on with someone who would be in their first trimester, it's why we also did the blood test. We won't know how far along you are until you get the blood test back, but I'm more than certain you're still in your first trimester."

I shook my head. "No. That can't be. Blaine and I are always careful."

Except for the time we weren't.

"I don't have a condom with me."

There were other things we could do to get off, but now that he had me on the brink, I just wanted him inside me. "Can you just pull out?"

"Are you serious?" I couldn't see his face, but I knew him well enough to know that his baby blues were probably wide with his eyebrows raised. The look he always gave me when he was shocked by what was coming out of my mouth.

I reached for his belt loops, pulling him closer. "Dead serious."

Shit. No. This couldn't be happening. Everything was going well. Perfect. I was going to finish school. Blaine wasn't afraid of commitment.

Holy shit, but it was.

The doctor went on talking and gave me some pamphlets as well as a number for a gynecologist in the area. I barely heard what she said because my brain was in a fog.

Pregnant. I was pregnant. With Blaine's kid.

I didn't know how I was supposed to tell him. Even worse, how was I going to tell my parents?

I BARELY REMEMBER THE drive home and by the time I got there, no one was home so I crawled into my bed and buried myself in the covers. It wasn't until then that I left myself cry.

I didn't know why I was crying. If it was some crazy pregnancy hormones or if I was just stressed and exhausted and it was all about to crash down on me.

I'd thought about having kids, but I always thought it would be later down the road when I was married and established in a career. Not when I was still struggling through college and afraid that any moment my boyfriend could have another melt down and leave me.

Now I was alone, crying in bed, and wondering how the hell I was going to take care of myself and another life growing inside of me.

Though I wasn't as alone as I thought.

A knock came at my bedroom door and I expected it to be Aunt Dee, but when the door creaked opened I looked up to see Blaine standing there with a brown paper bag in his hand.

He smiled as if nothing was wrong. As if our lives weren't about to change forever.

"Hey, baby. I stopped by the shop and Dee said you were still sick so I thought I'd bring you some chicken noodle soup from Sam's. It's supposed to be able to cure everything."

Pft. If he only knew.

"Thanks," I muttered and slowly sat up.

He placed the bag on my desk then sat down next to me on the bed. "Sorry for keeping you out so late last night. I guess I just got wrapped up in the birthday festivities."

"You're fine. I'm fine. It's fine," I said, even though I didn't mean any of it. I was way far from fine.

"So what did the doctor say?" Blaine asked.

I glared at him. "You don't want to know."

He laughed. "What, do you have mono and now we're both going to have the kissing disease?"

I groaned. All of the stress and sadness and confusion was now boiling up inside of me. I sat up and threw the covers, lifting my shirt off to expose my stomach. It was still flat but soon it would be the size of a house. "No. Blaine. I'm pregnant. Pregnant with your child. It's why I've been so sick lately and it's not going to get better for probably another seven months and then I'll have someone else to take care of."

His eyes widened as he stared down at my stomach. "You're shitting me."

I shook my head and put my shirt down. "No. I'm not shitting you. I'm pregnant. Knocked up."

He swallowed hard, his Adam's apple bobbing. "How? Are you sure?"

I rolled my eyes. "Yes, I'm sure. The doctor tested me. She said she'll have the blood test back soon to give me a closer approximation but I'm guessing around six weeks since that's when we had sex in the closet and you kind of didn't pull out."

He shook his head, his eyes still locked on my stomach. "I didn't know it could happen with just one time."

I glared at him, becoming more annoyed with each second passing. "Well, it did. I have to make a gynecologist appointment next week for an ultrasound. You can come with me or you can't. Either way, I'll figure it out. I always do."

"Libby. I don't really know what to say right now. What do you want me to say? I'm kind of in shock."

I felt the tears prick my eyes but I blinked them away. "Obviously you don't need to say anything. You're the first person I told. Now you should probably go so I can call my parents and tell them how I'm even more of a fuck up."

"Libby..."

"JUST GO!" I pointed at the door, the tears now fully streaming from my face.

"Okay." He nodded and his eyes stayed on the ground. "If that's what you want. I'll leave."

I didn't want him to leave. I didn't want to be alone, but I was such an emotional basket case that I wasn't sure if I could take it back. By the time I thought about yelling for him to take me in his arms, he was already gone, his truck pulling out of the gravel path.

I was alone. Utterly alone.

Except for the person that was growing inside of me.

I patted my stomach and looked down at it. "I don't know what I'm supposed to tell you or if you'll even hear me. That was just your daddy that left. He's a real good man, but I think he's scared. Scared like I am. I don't know what the hell I'm doing, but I can tell you this, I will do everything I can for you. No matter what. We're in this together."

Chapter 5

It was another hour before I finally got the courage to call my parents.

I didn't know what the hell I was supposed to say to them and when I called my mom, her voicemail kicked in.

It wasn't something that a daughter should leave on a voicemail so I just hung up.

That left talking to my dad.

I thought maybe I could talk to Aunt Dee or even Britt first, but deep down, I knew I had to tell him. Even if I felt like it may kill me to do so.

The phone rang three times and I breathed a sigh of relief, thinking it would go to voicemail and I'd have some time to think about what I was going to say. But on the fourth ring, he answered.

"Hey, Libby. How's it going?"

Shit. I didn't even know what I was supposed to say, so I blurted out the first thing I could think of. "How old are you going to be on your next birthday?"

"Hmmm...Well. It's in May and I think last year was my sixty-first, so coming up on my sixty-second. Why? Are you and Beth planning on making a cake?"

"Wow, that seems young to be a grandpa, don't you think?"

He laughed. "Well, I do have two grown daughters and Beth and Brian seem pretty happy."

"I meant a grandchild from me," I whispered.

"What was that?" he asked, a voice coming in somewhere in the background but he shushed it.

I took a deep breath and felt a tear slide down my cheek. "I'm pregnant, Dad. About six weeks."

The other end of the line was silent and I thought he'd hung up until I heard him breathing and his voice lowered. "You're joking."

I shook my head, even though I knew he couldn't see it. "No. I wish. I wish this was all a bad dream and I didn't mess up, again. I went to the doctor today and she gave me a pregnancy test and said I was positive. I go to a gynecologist next week."

"Have you told your mother?"

"No. Her phone went straight to voicemail."

He let out a deep breath. "I don't know what you want me to say, Libby. This is quite a shock, as you can imagine."

"I know. It is for me too. I don't want you to hate me or disown me, Dad. I didn't mean for this to happen," I cried.

"Well, there's no going back on it now. It may not be perfect. It may not be everything you thought it was, but it's happening. And we're having another grandchild. I have an afternoon appointment but I'll tell your mother to call you as soon as I see her."

His words were so final, as if he was just giving me a diagnosis like I was one of his dental patients. I sniffled, trying to grasp at what to say but I couldn't come up with anything.

"Okay, Dad. I'll wait for her call."

"Okay, Libby. And should I say congratulations?"

I thought on that one. I didn't know if I even felt like it was something worth congratulating or celebrating. "Sure. You can."

"Okay, honey. Well congratulations. I'll have your mother call."

"Bye, Dad."

"Bye, Libby."

And with that, he was off the phone. Like the whole thing had been some weird dream.

It wasn't long after that Britt came home from school. I wished it was just her, but since she wasn't getting her license for another few months, her friend Sarah was driving her around. And of course, Sarah had to come inside as well.

I was sitting at the kitchen table, figuring since I was eating for two now, it wouldn't kill me to eat some of Aunt Dee's pie that was in the fridge. So I was finishing up the last half.

"Whoa, Libby, take it you're feeling better," Britt said and dropped her book bag on the couch.

My little cousin lacked a fashion sense, but since she started hanging out with my gay friend Sawyer's hot, jock brother she started caring a little bit more about her appearance and wearing some lip gloss. She also exchanged her gym shorts and t-shirts in for jeans and started actually styling her pixie cut.

"Yeah. I'm eating for two, so at least I don't have to feel like shit when I eat this whole pie."

Libby and Sarah stopped and stared at me wide eyed.

Sarah took a step closer, her perfume and hair spray so thick that I thought I might puke from the smell. "Did you just say you're eating for two?"

I took the last bite of the pie, then licked the plate. "Yep. You're looking at the future first baby mama to Blaine Crabtree."

Britt shook her head. "Libby. That's not funny. It's a little early for April fool's jokes."

I laughed but there was no humor in it. "I wish it was an April fool's joke."

Britt took a tentative step forward. "Does Blaine know? Your parents? Grandma?"

"Ha. Yeah, Blaine was the first to know and he didn't stay long. He was more in shock than anything. My dad knows, but he didn't say too much. That just leaves my mom and Aunt Dee."

Sarah put a cold hand on my wrist. "Are you okay, honey? You seem a little...off..."

I laughed. "Yeah. I'm pregnant with my commitmaphobic boyfriend's baby, living in Louisiana with at least two years of school left, and, oh yeah, I'm sure my parents are discussing right now what my next form of punishment will be."

"Libby, they aren't going to punish you. A lot of people have kids before they're married and Blaine loves you. You'll both do the right thing, "Britt said.

"Yeah. Like I know what the right thing is," I muttered.

"You're not getting rid of it, are you?" Sarah gasped.

I shook my head. "No. I couldn't even if my crazy Catholic beliefs allowed it. For better or for worse, this little Crabtree is a part of me. Forever."

SARAH LEFT AND AUNT Dee came home a few hours later.

She had some grocery bags in her hands and set them on the counter. "Hi, Libby, what did the doctor say?"

I leaned against the counter, letting out a deep breath. "Well, it's not the flu."

"That's good. At least we don't have to worry about all of us catching it," Aunt Dee smiled and put some milk and cheese in the fridge.

"No, you can't catch this...I'm pregnant."

Aunt Dee stared into the open fridge, blinking once then twice before closing it. "Did I hear you right, honey?"

I bit my bottom lip, fighting back tears. God, I'd been crying too much. "Yes. I am."

"Oh, honey." She took me in her arms and held me as I cried. I didn't know if they were happy tears or if they were tears of sheer panic. Either way I was happy to have someone hold me and rub my hair, telling me it was going to be okay, even though I wasn't sure it was.

Aunt Dee let go of me but kept her hands on my shoulders. "Do you feel like eating? I have stuff for pecan pie."

Aunt Dee's answer for anything was always food. Food was usually my enemy, but I thought it couldn't hurt. I nodded and wiped my cheeks. "Yeah. That sounds great."

After I ate another half of a pie, my phone rang. I didn't know who I was expecting it to be, but when I looked down and saw my mom's name scroll across my screen, my heart dropped in my chest.

"I'm going to take this in my bedroom," I said, not waiting for an answer as I stood from the table and walked down the small hallway.

Once I was in my room I shut the door and swiped my phone to answer.

"Hey, Mom."

"Hey, Libby. Your dad told me I was supposed to call you and that you had something important to tell me?" She was breathless as if she just ran a few miles. She may have since she was getting into fitness now. Or she could have just been busy from running around the courtroom all day.

"Are you sitting down?"

"No, I'm standing in the kitchen, getting ready to order Chinese. What's up?"

I shook my head. "You should sit down."

"Okay. I'm sitting. What is it?"

I took a deep breath. "I'm pregnant. It's Blaine's. I know I'm not married and that this is the last thing you wanted to happen when I came down here. But it did. And I love him and I already love this thing in my stomach that is making me throw up all the time and I'm going to keep it. I don't know if Blaine will stick around and if he doesn't, oh well. I've grown a lot this past year and I know I can handle whatever life throws at me."

I didn't know where half of those words came from, but they all just spilled out of me.

Mom was silent for what seemed like forever before she finally spoke. "Wow. That wasn't what I was expecting, but I guess part of me knew this was going to happen eventually."

"Because I'm a screw up?" I tried to hold back the tears welling in my eyes.

"No, dear. Because you're in love. And sometimes these things happen when you're in love. I wish you two could have been married before this happened, but I understand it and I'm still going to love you and your baby and Blaine no matter what happens."

"Even if he leaves me? Even if I just end up some housewife with five kids and never live up to your expectations?"

"Libby, as long as you're happy and feel like you've succeeded, then that's all I can ask for you. When we first sent you down south it was a form of punishment, but as I watched you grow this past year, I knew it was more than that. And if this is where you're supposed to be and what you want, then I'm happy for you."

"But what if it isn't what I want?" I sniffled.

"Then you tell me what you want to do."

"I want to keep the baby, but I also want to finish school and to do all the things I've been planning on with my life for forever."

"Then what's stopping you?"

I thought on it for a moment. There were so many things swirling through my head that I didn't have an answer.

"I don't know."

"Well, then you can do them all. And if you need any help, we're here for you. Okay?"

I nodded. "Okay, Mom."

She asked a few more questions and I gave her the only details I knew. She didn't ask much about Blaine's involvement and I was happy not to talk about it.

"Okay. Now you should probably call your sister and then call me again after your next doctor's appointment."

"I will, Mom. I love you."

"I love you, too, Libby. Goodbye."

I hung up the phone and looked out my window. I didn't know when the day had turned into night, but there was a bright set of headlights coming in from the driveway.

Who would be visiting this late?

I really hoped that Aunt Dee didn't throw together some kind of impromptu "you're expecting" party and now her entire bridge club was coming over.

I sucked in a deep breath and headed out to the living room. Britt was at the kitchen table doing homework and Aunt Dee was putting up dishes.

"Are you expecting someone?" I asked, to both of them but it was more pointed at Aunt Dee.

Britt just shook her head but Aunt Dee came into the living room, looking out the front window. "Now who would be calling on us at this time of night?"

The front door of the car opened and I could barely make out the silhouette. It wasn't until he was at the front door that I recognized the blond head and bright blue eyes.

Blaine was back.

He rang the doorbell, even though I was pretty sure he could see me standing there near the front window.

"Who is it, honey?" Aunt Dee asked.

I sighed. "It's Blaine."

"Oh...Come on Britt. Let's head to the back for a bit. Give them some privacy," Aunt Dee said.

"Why? They won't even pay attention to us and I have to finish this worksheet."

"You can finish it later, just trust me."

Britt groaned but reluctantly followed. It wasn't until I heard the back door shut that I let out a big puff of air and opened the front door.

Blaine stood there looking every bit as disheveled as I felt with his hair spiking up all over the place. But his eyes. Oh his eyes. They still shone.

"Hey," he said.

"Hi."

"Mind if I come in?" he asked, raising his eyebrows.

"Yeah. Sure." I stepped back and let him walk into the house, shutting the door behind him.

He rubbed the back of his head, taking slow methodical steps until he was on the other side of me. "Sorry about earlier. I think I was kind of in shock."

"Uh, yeah, tell me about it." I walked past him and took a seat on the couch.

He followed and sat next to me, leaving a few inches of space between us. "It wasn't something I was expecting to hear. I mean, I thought someday it might happen, but we'd always been careful."

"Yeah, except the night of Britt's Cotillion," I scoffed.

"Right." He nodded.

It stayed silent for another few moments before I nodded my head out the window. "So when you left here, you decided to get a new car?"

He stared into space for what seemed like forever before he finally spoke. "Something like that."

"Gee, that makes me feel real good about our future. We fight and you go and buy a new car."

He shook his head. "I figured we'd need something that would be better for a family, so I traded my truck in for the Blazer."

He reached into his pocket and pulled out a small black box, setting it down on the coffee table. "And I used the rest of the money for this."

I eyed the box on the table before I picked it up, carefully examining it before opening it to reveal a white gold band with a round diamond sparkling from on top of it.

Blaine's hands were on my thighs as he got down on his knees in front of me. "I called your dad earlier today and asked his permission. I don't think he was happy about the whole situation, but I told him that I loved you and I knew this was going to happen someday, so it might as well be today. The day I ask you to be my wife and make our family whole."

I shook my head slowly, swallowing the lump in my throat. "Blaine, you don't have to do this just because I'm pregnant."

He let out a deep breath and put a hand under my chin, forcing my eyes to meet his. "You having my baby may have moved things along a lot quicker than we both would have liked, but that's not the only reason I'm down on my knees for you. I love you, baby. More than I've ever loved anything or anyone. Now please say you'll be my wife."

I bit my lip, chewing on it so hard I thought I was going to bleed. This wasn't what I was expecting, but looking into the vast blue of Blaine's eyes and thinking about the way he looked at me, I knew that it was where I was supposed to be. With him. Forever.

I smiled. "Of course."

Chapter 6

"**P**REGNANT WITH BLAINE'S KID?" Dina's eyes practically bugged out of her head.

"Shhh!" I put my finger to my lips. "There are customers."

Okay, there was only one guy milling around the shop, but she didn't have to yell it.

"Yes. It's going to be a shotgun wedding, I guess," I said, twirling the ends of my hair.

"What did your parents say?"

I shrugged. "Not too much. It's not like they were happy about me being pregnant."

Dina raised her eyebrows. "I mean about getting married. They aren't arguing that y'all are too young and you don't need to jump into anything just because you're pregnant?"

I shook my head. "Are you trying to tell me that?"

She waved her hands in front of her. "No, I'm not saying that at all, just something to think about. You know there are a lot of single mothers out there that are doing just fine and you do have a support system."

"I'm marrying Blaine. I love him. This would have happened sooner or later and I guess it's happening sooner," I snapped, harsher than I intended to.

Dina blew a breath of air out of her teeth. "No reason to be defensive with me, girl. When Jackson and I got serious, my daddy said all the same things. When we moved in together, he kept asking if I thought we were doing it too soon and if we were too young. I'm almost twenty-five years old."

She sighed. "But, you know, that's how parents think. They forget what it was like when they were younger, or they made stupid mistakes themselves and don't want to see us repeat them."

I bit my lip. "My parents didn't get married until they were out of law school and dental school, even though they had dated since they were eighteen."

Dina shrugged. "Well, that's what they did. It doesn't mean that's what you have to do."

I nodded. "Yeah, that's definitely not what we're doing."

Dina shook her head. "I never thought I'd see the day that Blaine Crabtree got hitched, let alone became a daddy."

"Well, you're going to see it because you're also going to be a bridesmaid and Jackson's going to be the best man."

Dina raised an eyebrow. "So, who is going to be the maid of honor?"

"My sister, duh. You know you'd be right up there and don't worry, she won't have eyes for Jackson. Unless my brother-in-law does something terribly wrong after she has her daughter next month."

Dina sighed. "Wow. This is all crazy. A baby. Getting married. Are you waiting until after the baby is born?"

I shook my head. "No. I wanted to but Blaine said he wanted us to actually be married whenever he or she was born and he wanted it to be on our dating anniversary. We're looking at June. We're actually meeting with the priest later this week."

Dina's eyes widened. "June? That's like four months away. How are you going to get everything done in time with school, a wedding, and you're not even done with your first trimester?"

"I have no idea."

AFTER DINA'S REACTION, I thought I could get away without telling people I was pregnant for a while...at least until my third trimester.

I'd been able to successfully avoid seeing Nikki, Blaine's ex-hook-up, for most of the semester. Even though we'd sort of made up in whatever our feud was, that didn't mean I wanted the reminder of seeing his ex every day.

But the one day, the one freaking day that my bladder failed me and I had to take a detour to the bathroom in the student union before heading to my class, I saw her.

I tried to turn in the other direction, but she caught me stepping out of the bathroom stall at the same time as her. Shit.

I cringed and tried to hide the grimace on my face as I turned toward her.

She looked every bit her practically-a-country-singer-good-looking-self with low slung jeans and a white tank top, her platinum blonde hair falling in loose waves on her shoulders. She was cute without even trying and it made it harder not to hate her.

"Hi, Nikki," I managed to force out.

"Hey. How you doing?" she asked, fiddling with the strap on her backpack.

I nodded. "Doing great, you?"

She walked in step with me as we exited the bathroom. I was hoping she would just answer and we'd be done, but I could never be that lucky.

"Doing good, doing good."

She was silent for all of two seconds before she finally sucked in a breath. "So Butch and I were over at Jackson's the other night."

"Cool." I didn't want to lead her, but I knew where it was going.

"And Dina said you and Blaine were engaged. Congrats."

"Yeah, he proposed the day after his birthday." I tried not to make eye contact with her. I didn't need to rub salt in the wounds and I also had a feeling that wasn't the end of her statement.

"Then Butch made a crack about you probably being pregnant if y'all were getting engaged so soon and then Jackson told us that y'all were, well, pregnant that is."

I stopped and she came to a halt beside me. I slowly turned toward her. "So you think that's the only reason Blaine would marry me? Because, let me tell you, he would have done it otherwise and you don't need to feel sorry or think we need to be besties now because I'm pregnant with your obsession's baby."

Nikki put her hands up. "Okay, first off, fuck you. I was trying to be nice, and second, I probably didn't say that in the best way, and I'll blame your reaction on hormones and my bitchiness."

I glared at her. I didn't know what to make of Nikki, ever. She was the type of girl that could probably kill a man with her bare hands and then have kinky sex with his best friend.

She sighed. "Look, Libby, I know I'm a bitch, I don't sugar coat it, but I'm not trying to say anything about you and Blaine. I just wanted you to know that I know. People are going to know. It's a small ass town. Some people are going to like it and some people are going to talk a hell of a lot of shit about it."

I raised an eyebrow. "And your point?"

She pushed her hair behind her ears. "I just wanted you to know that the Sinclairs have your back."

I nodded. "Okay. Well I appreciate that and I guess I'm sorry for my hormonal bitchiness too."

She finally smiled. "Now that this awkward conversation is out of the way, I have to go meet up with Butch. He wanted the details after I talked to you."

"Was he expecting me to be nine months pregnant and you would run to him and tell him that my water broke?"

She laughed, shaking her head. "No, I think he was hoping for a good girl fight, but I think we're both past that. And we both know I'd win."

"I don't know. I've got at least a foot on you and you wouldn't hit a pregnant woman."

"You're right. I guess you win."

I nodded. "I usually do."

She smirked. "That you do."

AFTER A FULL DAY OF class then work on Thursday, I wished I could have just slept the day away on Friday. But I had a feeling those days would soon be fewer and farther between.

And especially since Aunt Dee was able to get Blaine and I an appointment with the priest.

Like clockwork, every Sunday, The Crabtrees and Aunt Dee and Britt had been fixtures in the small Catholic Church in town. I knew we didn't have much of a choice in the matter of where we would be getting married and since Catholics couldn't get married outside, it was basically our only option unless we went back to Chicago. And there had been very little discussion about us having it anywhere other than Elsbury.

"Are you ready for this, Lib?" Blaine asked as we pulled into the church parking lot. We were the only other car there besides an old blue station wagon. I figured people would probably come later in the day to pray since it was Lenten season, but with it being early in the afternoon, it was empty.

I sighed. "I don't really have a choice, do I?"

Blaine shook his head and wiped the sweat off his forehead. He'd worked all morning on the road crew and picked me up at the shop right after lunch. He looked beyond exhausted with his dark circles and the fact that he yawned about a million times. "We don't have to do this. We can just run off to Vegas or the courthouse."

I laughed. "Yeah, that's definitely not an option."

"Who says so?"

"I do." I sighed. "I mean, I've never been the kind of girl that played dress up and dreamed of some grand wedding, but there's just something about the white dress and walking down the aisle with both our families being there to witness it that intrigues me. It's kind of what makes a marriage. The joining of two families."

He squeezed my knee. "And the beginning of ours."

"Yeah." I looked down at my stomach. "It is, isn't it?"

"I won't lie, it's been hard to wrap my head around everything. It's going so fast and I wish time could slow down, but at the same time it's exciting. It's like we get to take one giant leap forward into our future. No looking back."

I laughed. "Who are you and what have you done with my boyfriend? The Blaine Crabtree I know doesn't talk like that."

He opened the car door. "Your boyfriend isn't here. It's just your fiancé." He winked and went around the car, opening my door and helping me out.

I smiled. "And getting engaged turned you into a guy that loves commitment?"

He shrugged, swinging our intertwined hands between us. "Stranger things have happened."

We followed the cobblestone path up to the little white church. It reminded me more of a Southern Baptist church on a plantation than the grand cathedral-looking structures I was used to.

There was a doorbell next to the two carriage-style doors and Blaine buzzed it.

I thought we were going to have to wait forever. Father Donahue was not a young guy, by any means. I think he was older than my grandpa. So I was pretty damn surprised when he was at the door before the second ring went off. Not only that but he was in a baseball cap, an LSU shirt, and some muddy shorts.

"Hey y'all, sorry, I lost track of time working in the garden." His voice was always sugary sweet and inviting and I couldn't help but smile.

"That's fine. We should be apologizing to you since you had to meet us on such short notice," Blaine said, putting his hand on the small of my back as we stepped into the sanctuary.

"Would you two like to have our meeting in the garden? It's much better than sitting in my office and if we're lucky, maybe the birds will join us."

"Sure. That sounds great," Blaine said and we followed Father Donahue out the side door into the garden.

My parent's church back in the Chicago suburbs was meticulously landscaped; they had workers that came in just about every day to mow the lawn, water the flowers, and make sure everything was in place.

St. Alphonsus Church in Elsbury was definitely on a smaller scale and even though there was one line of flowers that flanked a side of the church and a few magnolia trees with benches beneath them, it was still easy to tell that it was well taken care of. Possibly all by Father Donahue himself.

Father Donahue took a seat on one of the benches and motioned for us to sit in the one across from it. "Sit a spell, would ya? And let's talk about how two of my younger members found love and want to spend the rest of their lives together. If I recall, y'all didn't meet too long ago?" He raised his eyebrows.

Blaine shook his head as we took the seat across from him. "No, sir. Since last June, which is why we were also looking at June for a wedding date. Our anniversary."

Father Donahue whistled through his teeth. "That's only four months away, son, and you know you're marrying a Yankee girl who I'm sure is going to want something big and fancy. Are you sure you don't want to wait until next June? Give some more time to plan?"

Blaine laughed. "It sounds like you're trying to talk us out of it, sir."

Father Donahue smiled and shook his head. "I just want to make sure you two aren't jumping into anything. There are a lot of young people that walk through these doors and promise God and their families that they'll be forever and then something happens and they break that vow. And it doesn't just affect them. It affects the church. Their families. Their world."

I swallowed hard. Plenty of my friends had parents who were divorced and Blaine and I both had our share of bad break ups, but it wasn't just about us anymore. There were three of us in the equation.

"Father, I love Libby Gentry. I've known that since the moment I laid eyes on her. I've sat in that church every single Sunday and every single Sunday I find myself staring at Libby across the aisle when I should be paying attention to your sermon. I know it's not very Christian of me, but I think I'd pay a whole lot more attention if this woman was at my side and my wife."

Father Donahue laughed and pulled out his phone. "Now you two are just trying to guilt me into it."

"Is it working?" Blaine asked.

Father Donahue was silent a few moments as he scrolled through his phone. "Well, I do have June 11th available. It's a Friday if y'all can do that. Now you'll have to get your Catholic marriage classes in before that and four meetings with me. So we'll need to get those booked as soon as possible. Do you think you two can handle that?"

Blaine looked at me and I squeezed his hand in response before looking at Father Donahue. "That sounds perfect. June 11th it is."

Chapter 7

Two weeks and morning sickness was still all day sickness.

I had my first appointment with an OB and I was hoping that she could give me something that would make me stop feeling so sick and drained all the time. I felt like I had a parasite that was just sucking the life out of me.

The doctor was in New Orleans, but not as far as the city. I made the appointment for a late Friday afternoon so Blaine would be able to get off of work and Aunt Dee was being very slack with my hours, which I was starting to feel bad about. It made me think about the future.

What the hell was I going to do about a maternity leave? Finish school with a child attached to my hip?

Growing up in such a short period of time was one hell of a ride and made me even more exhausted.

Blaine was supposed to pick me up at the shop when he was off work around two. He said he'd be done early. But when the clock struck 2:15, I found myself getting more and more agitated and every time I tried to call his phone, I just got a voicemail.

"Where the hell is he?" I muttered, staring out the shop window for the millionth time.

"Why don't you just go without him?" Marion, my older co-worker, asked from behind the counter.

Since I started she'd taken less hours at the shop, which I was glad for. It meant I didn't have to see her as much since she liked to be in my business. But with me working less hours with school, she ramped up her hours, which meant I was stuck with her constant prying.

"It's our first appointment and he said he'd be here."

She cackled. "Honey, haven't you figured out by now that you can't depend on a Southern man for anything more than fixing your car?"

She kept laughing like she said the funniest thing in the world. I looked at my phone and saw the time hadn't moved. Blaine still wasn't there and I had to get on the road.

I had to prove that my Southern man was worth more than fixing my car so I grabbed my purse from underneath the counter. "Tell Aunt Dee I'll be back later."

With that, I pushed open the door and got into my car, speeding as fast as I could to the construction on Parish Road.

The bright yellow trucks were on the side of the road, digging into the ground with orange cones and signs with the words 'Men Working' displayed for at least a mile.

I parked my car and jogged toward where a group of guys were standing around. It's not like they were in the middle of a big dig. They were just standing there with shovels in their hands and their bright yellow vests practically blinding me.

"Excuse me? Is anyone actually working?" I yelled, jogging up to them.

The guy with his back turned to face me and immediately his blue eyes lit up. Blaine was just freaking standing there when he knew how important this was to me.

"Hey, baby, you know you're not supposed to be here," he said, walking toward me and wiping the dirt on his jeans.

He was covered in dirt, even some flakes in his blond hair. There was sweat glistening from his forehead and I didn't doubt he was working. But not now. Not right freaking now.

"Yeah, you're not supposed to be here either. You were supposed to be at the shop half an hour ago," I spat.

His eyes widened and he wiped the sweat off his forehead. "Oh, shit, really? I'm sorry, baby. We've been trying to get this done."

I held my hands up. "Look, I don't want your excuses. You're either coming or you aren't."

"Baby, you know I want to come. Don't be like that."

I huffed. "Really? Because you were just standing around when I got here and it didn't look like you were working too hard."

He turned and pointed at the road behind him. "You see all that? You see the dug up road? The ones that my hands are all mangled from trying to expand? That's what I've been doing, so excuse me for taking five minutes to discuss the next moves with my team before we break for the day."

"No need to be an ass about it," I muttered, crossing my hands over my chest.

He turned, groaning as he shook his head. "I'm working my ass off here, Lib. We have a baby on the way and a wedding. I can't just stop working, if anything I need to work harder."

"What are you trying to prove? That you need to be a big man now?"

He rolled his eyes. "Are you going to get all feminist on me now that you're hormonal?"

I wanted to smack him. I even had my hands balled into fists, but instead I just stomped my foot like a little kid. "Argh! Whatever! I'm going to my appointment. Come if you want!"

I went to turn but he grabbed my arm, his grip firm. "Baby, wait. I'm sorry, okay? Don't get all mad at me. I'm just tired and I've been working in the sun all day. This is a stupid reason to fight."

"No. It's not. This is about us and you being late. Will you be late working when I go into labor as well?"

He groaned. "Libby, can we not argue about this now? Let's just get in the Blazer and get to your appointment."

I shook my head. "No. You don't have to go. I don't need you there. Go work, obviously that's more important."

He put his other hand on my arm and looked into my eyes. "Baby, do you know how important you are to me? You and our baby. It's why I'm working my ass off. Things are just going to get crazier as spring moves into summer. You know this. It was like this last summer, I just tried not to work as much overtime so I could spend more time with you. I don't have that luxury now and I want to do the time now so that when the baby comes, I'll have the flexibility if I need to scale back with work."

I blinked. "Do you really mean you're going to scale back?"

"If I need to. I'm in this with you, Lib. I need to get all this work out while I can and then if you need me to hold your hand or run out in the middle of the day to get diapers, I can do that. Okay?"

I sucked in a deep breath. I knew this wasn't going to be the last of our arguments, but for now I'd take it. "Okay."

BLAINE PULLED THE CAR up to a brick building with a small pink sign that said "Obstetrics and Gynecology" in a very swirly font.

"Well, that's welcoming," Blaine said and smirked, putting the car into park.

"Get used to it, Blaine. If we have a girl, it's going to be all pink and glitter." I smiled.

"I hope you and your mama aren't planning the same thing with our wedding."

I cringed and hoped he didn't notice. No such luck.

He raised an eyebrow. "You still haven't told her our plans for the wedding yet have you? Does she think it's going to be up in Chicago in two years at a country club? Or does she think we won't actually do it and you'll end up back there living in the guest room?"

"Blaine! Why do you say things like that?" We'd just gotten done having an argument and I wasn't ready to have another one.

He sighed. "I don't know. I guess because I'm nervous and worried and I'm about to walk into a place where my fiancée is going to have her legs strapped up and some woman feeling her lady parts."

I laughed. "Well, at least you're honest."

"I'm serious, baby. This all scares the shit out of me."

I squeezed his hand. "Yeah, I'm scared as hell too. But we have to be in this together. We both can't run and hide or nothing is going to get done."

He nodded. "Yeah, I guess I need to stop acting like a sissy and man up, ey? Our son is going to need that."

I smirked and opened the car door. "Or our daughter. I'm thinking we should go with a traditional name. Maybe Glimmer."

He got out of the car and followed me around to the front. "Like hell. If anything, she'll have a Southern belle name like Scarlett O'Hara Crabtree."

I put my arm around his waist and leaned my head on his shoulder. "At least you're getting used to the idea of a girl."

He put his arm around my shoulder and squeezed it before opening the glass door in front of us. "A girl who plays softball."

The waiting room looked more like someone's living room than any doctor's office I'd ever been in. The walls were painted a mint green color with different black and white portraits of families on the walls. Instead of uncomfortable waiting room chairs, there were plush, modern brown sofas with tables that looked like they were made out of pallets and flanked each side of the sofas.

The opposite side of the room had a large, brown desk with glass lighting pendants that dropped down just a few feet from the receptionist's heads.

Blaine and I approached the desk where two smiling ladies sat in pink scrubs. One was on a computer and the other one on the phone. I didn't know which one I was supposed to approach so I just stood there with my hands together until the woman on the phone looked at me.

"How can I help you, honey?" Her accent wasn't as thick as some other women in Louisiana but it still made me smile.

I stepped closer to the desk. "Hi, I'm Elizabeth Gentry and I have an appointment with Dr. Miller."

The woman looked over at her computer and typed a few things in. "Okay, I have you checked in but I'm just going to need you and your husband to fill out a few forms here."

Husband? Did she just really say that?

She grabbed a few papers and put them in a clipboard and handed it to me with a pen. "It's just some basic family history, HIPAA, and medical history. If you don't finish it all before you get called back, you can finish it in the room or just hand in what you have."

I was going to correct her on calling Blaine my husband, but instead I just smiled, took the clipboard, and took a seat on one of the couches. Blaine sat next to me and fidgeted every few seconds while I tried to fill out the form.

Finally I couldn't take it anymore. "Is everything okay? Are you upset because she called you my husband? Or is this still about our argument, because now isn't the time to bring it up," I whispered.

He laughed and shook his head, licking his lips. "No. I'm not upset about that at all...but..."

"But what?" I raised an eyebrow.

He lowered his voice. "This place is just a little weird is all. All the magazines have pregnant women on them and the pictures are of half-naked women. There isn't a Sports Illustrated or anything in sight."

I laughed. "Really? Did you think there would be?"

He shrugged. "Hey, a lot of guys come in here with their women. They need reading material too."

"I'll be sure to tell the doctor that."

As if the staff knew we were talking about them, the door near the front desk opened and a short, younger woman in pink scrubs called my name.

"Looks like you can tell him right now," Blaine said and nudged my side as we stood up.

"Smart ass," I muttered.

"Are you Mr. and Mrs. Gentry?" The woman asked as we approached the door.

"It's Miss Gentry, for now, this is my fiancé, Blaine Crabtree," I said.

She nodded, her smile fading a bit. "My apologies."

I knew there would be people that judged us for having a kid and not being married. I didn't expect it at a doctor's office, but I guess it did happen. Maybe it was better to get married before he or she was born...as long as we made it without too many more fights.

"It's no problem," I said.

"Okay, well, why don't you two follow me back to ultrasound?"

She shut the door behind Blaine and me and led us down a small hallway that had closed doors on each side.

"An ultrasound? Am I far enough along for that?" I asked.

The woman nodded and looked at her paperwork. "This helps the doctor get a better idea of how far a long you are and then we go from there assessing your due date and pre-natal care. After we get some pictures, then you'll meet with the doctor. Is that all right?"

I shrugged. "Do I have a choice?"

The woman laughed and opened a door to a dark room. In one corner, there was a computer screen with a chair that had large silver stirrups attached to it.

"Mr. Crabtree, you can sit on the chair next to the station there, and Miss Gentry, I'll have you hop up on this chair." The woman patted the chair with the stirrups.

"Okay." Blaine and I did as she asked before she took a seat on a wheeled stool and pulled up to the computer screen, typing a few things in on the keyboard.

"All right Miss Gentry, I'm going to have you lay back and scoot so that your butt is at the end of the seat, then roll up your shirt."

"Okay." I did so and she took some paper towels and put them on my lap, stuffing the tops into the waistband of my jeans.

"Now I'm going to use this warm gel and spread it across your stomach with this wand, then we'll be able to see your little peanut on the screen," she said, squirting the warm jelly on my stomach.

She typed a few things with the keyboard with one hand and then pressed the wand down on my stomach with the other. Within a few seconds, the speakers blared a swirling sound that sounded like treading water. On the screen popped a black image surrounded by shades of gray and in the middle of all the black was a small, lima bean shaped gray blob. My blob.

"Is that the baby?" Blaine asked, staring over my shoulder.

The woman nodded. "That would be the future little Crabtree."

The woman pressed a few more buttons on her keyboard and then pointed at the screen. "You can see the head and formation of the spine and even some little buds for arms." She pointed at the screen and enlarged it.

"He looks like a little tadpole," Blaine said.

"Did you just refer to our daughter as an amphibian?" I asked, staring up at him.

Blaine looked down at me and smiled before placing a chaste kiss on my lips. "Nope. Just stating that she gets her looks from her daddy."

He grabbed my hand and squeezed it before looking back at the screen. "It's really real. All of this. We're having a baby."

I nodded, biting my bottom lip to keep myself steady and not try and have an emotional outburst of happy tears. "Yes. We really are."

The woman typed a few more things on the keyboard and some lines appeared near the baby. "And it looks like we're measuring around eight weeks, so that would put your due date at the end of September. I hope the Saints have a bye that weekend."

Blaine laughed. "Even if they don't, I'm sure our baby would like to be introduced to the world with the Saints playing in the background."

The woman laughed and printed out some small prints of the ultrasound and handed them to me. "I'm sure the doctors would like that too."

I stared down at the prints. The first portraits of the little thing that had been giving me hell for weeks and now it was real. Really real. And in September, I'd be holding that baby in my arms with Blaine by my side as my husband.

When I left Illinois, I never thought any of this would ever happen and now that it was, I knew it was exactly where I was supposed to be.

AFTER MEETING THE DOCTOR and discussing pre-natal care, Blaine and I went back out to the car with a load of vitamin samples, brochures, and magazines to read through. It was going to be a long thirty-two weeks.

When I got in the car, I finally pulled out my phone and saw that I had three missed calls from my mom.

"Hey, baby, do you mind if I call my mom?" I asked Blaine as he got into the car.

He shook his head. "No, that's fine. I should probably call my mama, too, or we can stop by there before I drop you off at home."

"Yeah. That sounds great."

I dialed back my mom's cell phone and she answered on the second ring. "Libby! Where have you been?"

"Sorry, I was at a doctor's appointment. Your grandbaby should be here at the end of September."

"Oh good! That will definitely give us time for the opening at the country club next June. The priest said you two could meet with him when you come here in March, but he's basically already said we could have that date."

Shit. This is what Blaine and I had talked about. I needed to tell my mom that we wanted to get married here and in a few months. I'd been putting it off for too long. But I guess it was now or never.

"Actually...Mom...Blaine and I have been talking and we were kind of thinking of getting married this June...you know...before the baby is born."

"In three months? I don't know if I'd be able to get the church then. You know these things book up years in advance."

I sighed and looked at Blaine who smiled at me, trying to give me some sort of courage. "Actually, we've already talked to the priest here. We want to get married in Elsbury."

Mom was silent for a few moments before she spoke again. "You don't want to get married in your hometown? What about everyone that will have to travel?"

I ran my fingers through my hair, twirling the ends. "It's just...this is where I feel the most comfortable. It's where I've gone to church every Sunday these past nine months. It's where my child will be raised."

My parents and I still hadn't discussed what would happen after the baby was born. I think they knew there was no way I was moving back to Illinois, especially with marrying Blaine, but now it was all out there in the open.

"Okay, well, I'll make some calls then, but I have to run to a meeting. I'll talk to you soon." Before I could get in another word edgewise, Mom hung up.

I let out a deep breath and tossed my phone in my purse.

"Went that well, ey?" Blaine said, squeezing my hand.

"Well, she didn't say no," I said.

Blaine shook his head. "She really couldn't. We are adults and this is what we both want."

"Yeah, but my parents have done everything for me. I mean they're paying for my school right now and they've supported everything."

"Yeah, but that's going to change. You and I both know that, and we both have to do what's best for our little family and what we want. If I have to work any more hours, I can do that. We'll make it work." He patted my stomach.

"You're probably right, but that doesn't make it suck any less when I hear her disappointment."

"She'll come around, baby. Don't worry. And if she doesn't, well then I guess I get to add another guest to my side of the guest list."

I glared at him. "Don't start with the guest list."

He laughed. "Okay, how about with what you're putting on my grooms' cake? I'm thinking an LSU crawfish theme."

I shoved his shoulder. "You're lucky I love you."

He smiled and kissed my cheek. "And I'll never stop."

Chapter 8

I loved my car. Loved it.

A red BMW convertible was what I'd dreamed about since I was a little girl. My dad okayed it since it was a reliable car and I had decent grade in high school. Now, four years later, I wasn't living with my parents or in Chicago. I was about to have a baby, so a two door convertible was not the best car for me.

I had to give it up.

I'd been looking online for a few days, but nothing really caught my eye. Okay, so maybe the Mercedes SUV that my sister had was really calling to me, but I wasn't exactly sure that I could spend that much on a car.

Blaine and I planned to spend the day on Saturday car shopping, so I picked him up at his place where he was already on the front porch waiting.

"You know this would be a lot easier if we were living at the same place," I said as he got into the passenger seat.

"One step at a time, baby. One step at a time."

I groaned, but didn't want to argue at that moment. We'd had the discussion a million times before, but now it was getting serious. I didn't exactly want to live out of my Aunt Dee's guest room or in his parent's attic while we were married and had a kid. But he seemed to think there was a lot of other stuff we had to get situated first. Like a car.

"Turn up here, baby," Blaine said, pointing out the front window.

"Aren't we going into New Orleans?" I asked, raising an eyebrow.

"Not yet. Bubba called me this morning and said he has a friend that's been trying to sell his car for a while and thinks we might be interested."

I scoffed and shook my head. "I don't want to buy some random dude we don't even know's car. What if he smoked in it? What if it has a million miles on it? What would we do with my car? Just keep it for our Sunday drive care and use our little savings to buy some hunk of junk?"

Blaine sighed. "Baby. Just look at it. Bubba says it's nice and if we like it, we could put your car up for sale on the lot near Sam's Drive-In."

"Really? Just sell my car to someone on the street for a few grand? Why don't we take it to the dealership and see what they'll give us for a trade-in?"

Blaine groaned. "Because the dealership is going to rape us. They'll give us a few grand for this and then try and sell us some overpriced foreign SUV and you'll probably jump on it."

"And what if that's what I want?"

"Is your daddy going to pay for it like he has for everything else? Because I sure as hell don't want to keep working overtime forever to keep you in luxuries," Blaine snapped.

I slammed on my brakes and pulled over to the side of the road. Luckily there were no cars because I was pretty sure I left some marks in the road from moving so fast. "What the hell?"

Blaine rubbed the back of his neck and looked at me. "I'm just saying, you're used to your parents paying for things and now that we have to do it on our own, I think we should just be a little smarter with our money. If we could get a good price for your car and get a cheaper, but reliable car for you, we'd have some money for our other expenses."

It could have been a reasonable argument if I wasn't so hormonal and if the way he said the words didn't sound so judgmental. "So, you think because I'm some spoiled little rich girl that now I have to give up everything, when I've already given up a lot including my body, to make sure everything fits into how you want it?"

He held up his hands. "Now, baby, I didn't say that."

"Then what are you saying?"

He sighed and shook his head. "Let's just forget about it. We can go see Bubba another day. Let's go to New Orleans and see what they have for you at the dealership."

I shook my head. "No. I don't want to go."

"Baby, please don't be like this," he pleaded.

I held back the tears. I was always a crier, but now it was worse. I felt like I could cry over spilled milk. "I'm not ready to do this right now. Let's forget about it and I'll take you back home."

"Baby..."

I put the car back in drive and did a U-turn, heading back toward his parents'. "Not now, Blaine. We can talk about this later. Talk about everything later."

He opened his mouth to speak and then shut it again. "Okay, Libby. If that's what you want."

Then he didn't say another word the whole way to his house and only kissed my cheek before getting out of the car.

Part of me wanted to yell at him to get back in, but the other part of me knew that I needed some space before I went on another hormonal rage.

SAWYER HAD TEXTED ME earlier in the day. He was one of the few friends I'd made at school and we planned our semester around each other's so we could study together. I figured if I wasn't going car shopping with Blaine, then I could meet him at the coffee shop near campus to study for our history midterm.

"You sure you should be drinking that?" Sawyer asked, raising his eyebrows as I took the seat across from him with my steaming mug.

I rolled my eyes. "Yes, Sawyer. I can have one cup a day. Geez, are you my mother now?"

"Well, when one of my best girls texts me and tells me she's knocked up by her man candy, I figure she needs to learn some Southern manners."

I pouted. "Sorry. Should I have sent you a telegram? Is that how all the belles do it?"

He shook his head and took a sip out of his own cup. "Not that I know of, but next time you tell me in person, okay?"

I sighed and pulled my notebook out of my bag. "If there will ever be a next time. This first time is already killing me."

"Lady troubles?"

I shook my head. "I wish. More like man troubles. Blaine just doesn't get things and with everything moving so fast. Sometimes I feel like I can't catch my breath, and I'm looking for him to help but he's drowning just as bad as I am."

"Then maybe you should try and slow it down."

I sighed. "I wish. Wedding in June, which my mother still is refusing to talk to me about, baby due in September, and I've got this semester to finish plus I still have a full schedule of classes this summer."

He nodded, raising his eyebrows. "Well, that is a lot."

"That's not even the half of it. We had our doctor's appointment and he is freaking late because he's working overtime. I had to drive across town to pick him up and he was just standing there on the site, shooting the shit with his crew. Then, we tried to go car shopping today, because obviously that's more important than us finding a place to live together, and he wanted me to get some junker from Bubba Sinclair. It's like, he just does what he wants and forgets that I'm in this too. Hell, I'm the one carrying the baby."

Sawyer raised his eyebrows. "Do you think that's how he feels?"

I shrugged. "I don't know. It sure as hell seems like it."

Sawyer put his hand on mine. "Honey, I say this because I love you, but you know that Blaine is just a good ol' Southern boy. He's just doing what he's always known. You know he's just as scared as you are so he's doing the best he can and trying to figure it out alongside you. Cut him a little bit of slack."

"Why do you always have to take his side?"

Sawyer smiled. "Hey, the man's gotta have somebody. I'm sure whenever you pop out little Sawyeretta, he'll be out numbered."

I laughed. "Sawyeretta? You just come up with that on your own?"

He shook his head. "No, I thought on that one for awhile. It's a good name."

"Well, I'll make sure to tell Blaine about that one."

"So you're not going to stay mad at him and become some angry single mom?"

I smiled. "You know I can never stay mad at the good ol' Southern boy for long."

Sawyer nodded. "Good and cut him some slack on working. You know I love watching him come up on his momma's porch all sweaty from a day's work and then rip off that shirt like some kind of country music video boy."

I raised my eyebrows. "Do you just hang out with me to watch him?"

He laughed. "Sometimes."

I sighed. "It just sucks. He's working all the freaking time."

"But isn't it road construction season? All I see are them boys on the side of the road when I'm on my way to school and work."

"Maybe," I grumbled.

"And shouldn't he be working more hours since you're working less and going to school more?"

I threw my pen at Sawyer. "Stop taking his side already. I get it!"

He grinned and took a sip of his coffee. "Just making sure, darlin.'"

AFTER A FEW HOURS AT the coffee shop, I headed home. I was going to call Blaine and apologize for being such a brat, but when I pulled into the driveway, his car was already there. When I got out of my car, I saw him sitting on the front porch with a bouquet in his hands.

I smiled and walked up to him. "Flowers again for an apology?"

He smiled and stood up, holding the bouquet out to me. "No. Baby socks."

I took the bouquet and looked at it. Instead of a dozen roses they were rolled up white baby socks, made to look like tiny flowers. "Oh my god! This is the cutest thing I've ever seen!"

He rubbed the back of his head. "Yeah, the lady at the flower shop had this on display and I couldn't resist. I also thought it would be a way of letting you know how important you two are to me and I need to stop being such a stubborn ass sometimes."

I shook my head and set the bouquet down on the porch. "I'm sorry for being a hormonal bitch, too. Sawyer already gave me enough grief about it. If you want to go look at cars again this week, I may be willing."

Blaine put his arms around my waist and pulled me closer. "Actually, I was thinking we should check out this duplex first. It's over by your school and would only be about a five mile extra commute for me to get to the job site."

I put my arms around his neck and raised my eyebrows. "Are you serious?"

He nodded. "Serious as sin, sweetheart. I thought about what you said and I know we have a lot of shit going on and should take this one step at a time. But, I think this is a big step we both need to take and it would be a lot easier if we're living together."

I licked my lips. "That's very true."

He leaned in, biting his bottom lip. "And have some actual alone time that would be much appreciated before the baby comes."

I leaned in and smiled. "That's even truer."

He placed a quick kiss on my lips. "So are you going to let me take you to see the new place or want to head out and look at cars?"

I pouted. "Can't I just enjoy being in your arms for a few seconds longer?"

He laughed. "Well, usually I'd oblige, but I'm pretty sure your little cousin is looking through the window at us right now."

I looked behind Blaine and the curtains moved quickly. He was definitely right.

I let go of his neck and took his hand. "Well, then I guess we'd better go find our own place."

Chapter 9

My first trimester was coming to an end and I was exhausted. Blaine and I had looked at four different places and none of them were going to work for us. They were either too far for him or too far for me. Small bedrooms or not enough storage. The list went on and on.

I was starting to think that maybe moving into his parents' wasn't such a bad idea if we couldn't agree on anything.

I also still had work and school. Aunt Dee had been giving me less hours at work, which was fine since she wasn't paying me right now, but I knew once I moved out and wasn't getting the free rent, I'd need the paycheck and couldn't keep going at this pace.

Luckily, I had a counselor appointment in the morning before work. I thought maybe she could shed some light to help my situation.

One of the agreements I made with my parents, when I left the hospital and was able to stay in Louisiana, was that I had to see a nutritionist and counselor. I'd been working mainly online with the nutritionist, even throughout the pregnancy, but I couldn't exactly phone in the counselor.

Her office was about twenty minutes from Aunt Dee's house in a small strip mall that was wedged between a dentist office and a general practice. It wasn't anything special and the waiting room definitely wasn't as lavish as the one at the gynecologist's office, but it served its purpose.

I checked in at the front desk and after only a few minutes, my counselor was calling me back.

Ophelia Granger was a very tall woman. Taller than me. She also had long black dreadlocks strung with different beads that always coordinated with her colorful maxi dresses. Her office was full of different tribal accents and she always had sage or something burning. At first I was kind of weirded out by the whole thing, but the longer I sat with her, the more I liked her.

She took a seat behind her desk and I sat on the brown leather couch in front of it. "So, tell me, Libby, what's new?"

"Well, besides hating this first trimester of pregnancy, studying for midterms, getting engaged, and trying to find a new place to live with Blaine; not much."

Her eyes practically bugged out of her head and she leaned forward. "Let's back that up a bit. Pregnant? Engaged? When did this all happen?"

I bit my bottom lip. "Right after I saw you last I found out I was expecting, due in September. Then Blaine proposed and wants to get married in June. My mom isn't exactly happy with it. No one in my family really is."

She nodded. "But are you happy?"

It was an honest question, so I gave an honest answer. "Yes and no. More like overwhelmed."

She smiled. "That seems to be your thing. You always have so much going on and have trouble trying to stop and enjoy it. With this much going on your life right now, you really do need to take some time to breathe."

"Ha! Maybe in another year and a half when I finish my associates, but by then I'll have a toddler and probably be pulling my hair out."

She crossed her arms over her chest. "You know if you talk like that, you're just setting yourself up to fail. Have you thought about the positives instead of all of the negatives?"

I sighed. "Of course not. Sometimes it's hard to see them."

"Do you have a man who loves you?"

I nodded. "Well, yeah."

"And you're still doing well in school?"

"As well as I can."

She smiled. "See, those are some positive things. I think you need to try and focus more on those instead of always worrying about the negatives. I know it's hard for you, but instead of looking at 'Oh, I'm exhausted,' look at the positive part of it. 'I'm exhausted because I'm growing a baby and it gives me a good excuse to take a nap in the middle of the day'. "

"I guess I can try that."

"You'd better. It's your homework for this week."

I raised an eyebrow. "You're giving me homework now?"

"Think of it in a positive way. It's more like practice for seeing the positives when your baby spits up over your new dress and you need an outlet."

AFTER ANOTHER HALF an hour of laughing and talking to Ophelia, I felt a little bit better about everything. That is until I saw a missed call from Kristi on my phone.

I hadn't talked to her in weeks and it was mostly just random texts or comments on Facebook. I still hadn't told her about being pregnant. She knew I was engaged, but not the reasoning behind it. Maybe she wanted to wedding chat over the phone and not through text?

I slid in my car and closed the door before dialing her number.

"Guess where I am?" she asked in a sing-songey voice.

"Um, at work?"

"If by work you mean a business trip to New Orleans, then yes!"

"Oh! I didn't know you were coming here." I chewed on my bottom lip.

"It was sort of a last minute thing, so I'm hoping you can take a lunch break and meet up with me? Where's the best place that's close to the Wyndham in the French Quarter?"

This was the last thing I wanted to do today, but I was trying to look at the positive. I guess I could tell Kristi in person about being pregnant and it would be nice to see her again.

"There's a great bistro on Royal Street. I can be there in about forty-five minutes if traffic isn't bad and I can find parking."

"Sounds great. I'll see you then!"

I hung up the phone and let out a deep breath before starting the car. At least I had some time to mentally prepare to tell another person about the hot mess that was my life.

KRISTI ALWAYS LOOKED so put together. I could have spotted her from a mile away as soon as I walked into the restaurant. She had her red hair styled in a French twist and her makeup was flawless, even when the weather was starting to heat up.

"Libby! You're here! You look great!" She stood up and hugged me. I tried to smooth out my maxi dress and not look so frumpy next to the girl in the gray skirt suit, but there was no use. I was bloated and tired and probably really looked like I just rolled out of bed.

"You look even better," I said, letting go of her and taking the seat across from her as she sat back down.

"I wish I felt better. It's been crazy. I'm just happy to be out of meetings!"

"Yeah, I know the feeling of being crazy," I muttered.

"Well, yeah! You're planning a wedding! Let me see that diamond. Facebook didn't do it justice!'

I put my hand out and she examined the ring on my finger. It wasn't like the two carat one that Gabe gave her, but I still loved it.

"So, what's the plan for the wedding? Your parents' church, then the country club?" She asked.

I bit my bottom lip. "Not exactly. We're hoping to have it here. Well, not here, here. But in Elsbury, at the Catholic Church there, then the reception at Blaine's parents' house."

"Oh my god! A real Southern wedding! That actually sounds awesome!"

"Yeah. I hope you're free this June because I'll need a bridesmaid." I smiled.

Her face fell. "Well, of course I'll be there. It's not like I have much else going on but work."

She smiled again and took a sip of her water, but I knew something was off.

"Is everything okay?" I raised an eyebrow.

She sighed and shook her head. "I don't want to burden you with anything, but. Ugh."

She ran her fingers over her hair. "I know I just got married and I shouldn't be worried about these types of things, but I went off the pill after the wedding, not planning anything but thinking if it happened then it happened. Well nothing has happened. I'm freaking barren. I went to my gynecologist and she said that it could take a while, but if we aren't pregnant within a year of trying, we could do some tests on both of us and possibly start medication. The hell? Like why does this have to happen? Why tests and medication and all this shit when some teen girl can get knocked up the first time she doesn't use a condom and then end up with a reality TV show?"

I blinked, absolutely speechless at her words.

She shook her head. "I'm sorry, that was really harsh of me, but it's how I'm feeling and I just needed to vent. Everyone is getting pregnant and married or getting new jobs and I'm over here working sixty hours a week and complaining about those damn high school kids."

"No. It's totally fine. Sometimes you need to vent to a friend."

I didn't even know what to say after that. Luckily, Kristi kept talking and when the waiter came and took our order, I was ready for the welcomed break to choke down my water as fast as I could.

But then Kristi's drink order came.

"Here, do you want to try this? It's delicious. It tastes like lemonade and you can't even taste the alcohol." She held the drink in front of me.

I shook my head. "No thanks. We're out in public and you know I have to drive home."

She rolled her eyes. "Oh, please. One sip won't kill you. I'm having a drink with lunch and it's a business trip. We all need a little relaxer."

"No, really. I'm fine. I don't need it."

"What, are you on another diet? Does your nutritionist know?"

I shook my head. "No. I just don't want a sip."

"Come on, Lib. Peer pressure! Don't make me sing a Kappa drinking song in the middle of a restaurant."

"Kristi, no. Really. I'm fine."

"Drink a beer. Drink a beer. Drink a G—"

"Kristi, I can't have a drink because I'm pregnant!" I blurted out, cutting her off mid-sentence.

She blinked, staring at me wide-eyed as she set the glass down. "You're what?"

I sighed. "I'm pregnant. It's why Blaine and I got engaged and why we're getting married this summer. We haven't told a lot of people outside of our families. I was going to tell you earlier but then you started talking about fertility issues and I just didn't know how to bring it up."

"Wow..." She stared off into space.

"Yeah. I know. Sorry it came out like that."

She shook her head. "No. It's totally cool. I understand."

I just nodded. I didn't think she did, but I didn't know what else I was supposed to say or how I was supposed to find the positive in that.

And I guess she didn't know what to say either, because for the rest of lunch we just made small talk about the weather and New Orleans. There was no talk of babies or weddings. She gave me a quick hug when we were done with lunch and we went on our separate ways, as if that was it. I kind of thought it might have been. I didn't know if she'd want to be around someone who was pregnant when she was struggling and I didn't know if I could blame her, but it still hurt.

I got into my car and saw a text from Blaine

How was lunch?

I responded quickly before setting my phone back in my purse and heading back toward Elsbury.

Okay. Kristi told me she was having fertility problems and I blurted out that I was pregnant. So actually it sucked.

I heard a buzz from the passenger seat, but didn't bother picking up the phone. Blaine had given in to going to the dealership and we traded my convertible in for a modest sedan. It wasn't exactly my favorite car in the world, but we worked it out to have a very small payment and it was brand new. I also got a sunroof out of the deal so if I couldn't have the top down, at least I could have a little bit of a breeze to cool me down on the road back to Elsbury. The breeze sort of kept my mind off of the terrible lunch. Sort of.

Instead of going to Aunt Dee's, since I only had an hour before work started, I decided to stop at Sam's Drive-Thru and get a root beer float. I also grabbed a few bottles of water and headed toward the site Blaine was working at.

I pulled on the side of the road and parked behind a few trucks.

"Hey, Blaine, your baby mama is here!" A guy yelled as soon as I got out of my car.

I rolled my eyes and stopped where the road block barricade started. "I won't take up too much of his time."

Blaine came jogging toward me and smacked the guy on the back before wiping his brow. "Thanks, Bud. I'll only be a few minutes."

"Hey, babe, what's up?" Blaine asked breathlessly before he pulled his shirt up and wiped his face. He was sweating so badly it looked like he just got out of the shower, but I couldn't deny that I still took a peek at his V line and the contours of his bronzed abs when he lifted his shirt. It'd been awhile since we'd done anything sexual and the more time he spent at work, the more defined his body got. I couldn't help but take notice. See? Positives.

"Not much. Just got done with lunch with Kristi and thought I'd bring you some water before I headed to work," I said and handed him a bottle.

He took it and opened it, chugging half of it and then poured the rest over his face. The water dripped over his skin, soaking his t-shirt, leaving only a few droplets on his lips and the ends of his hair. I wanted to kiss off every single one of them. "Yeah, your text made it sound like your lunch was brutal."

"Yeah. It was." I leaned against the post.

Before Blaine could say another word, Jackson came running up to us, running his hands through his red beard that was definitely in need of a trim. "Hey, Lib, how ya doing?"

"I'm good, Jackson, how are you?"

He nodded. "Good, well I was, until I saw something on Facebook."

Blaine smacked his chest. "Man, what are you doing on your phone when we need to get this shit done?"

Jackson rubbed the back of his head. "Well, I wouldn't have been if Dina didn't text me like there was some kind of an emergency, so then I had to see the drama for myself."

I raised an eyebrow. "Is there something I should be worried about?"

Jackson blew out a breath between his teeth. "Well, your little red headed friend may or may not have tagged you to announce to the whole world that her little sister was getting married in June and then the thread after that may or may not have eluded to you being pregnant."

"What?" I snapped and pulled my phone out of my pocket.

I pulled up the Facebook app and there it was, the tagged post.

Lunch with my little sister. Super excited for her wedding this June! Yes THIS June!

Then I did the stupid thing and read through the comments.

Wow! That's really soon? Is she knocked up?

Probably. What else is there to do there but tip cows and make babies?

And of course Kristi's comments.

I'm not saying anything, but you may want to ask the lil mama and papa :)

This was the last way that I wanted to tell the world. How could she do that?

I didn't even know I was crying until Blaine was wiping a tear from my cheek. "Hey, baby. What did she say? Is everything okay or do I need to have a talk with someone?"

I shook my head. "Kristi just put up a post about having lunch and basically told the world I was pregnant. Why would she do this?"

Jackson patted Blaine's back. "I'll give you two a minute."

Blaine walked around the blockade and stood in front of me. He took my phone and set it down on the ground before looping his arms around my waist. "Some people just can't be happy for others. Maybe this was her way of dealing with her own drama. It'll all pass over, but it's not our concern. Now people know and they can either support us or they can go screw themselves. All that matters is that you and I are happy."

"I guess that's true."

He kissed my forehead. "There's no guessing. It is."

I smiled. "Okay. It is."

"Now, since we have an hour before you go to work...if you did want to get in a quickie, I'm sure Jackson could cover for me"

I swatted his chest. "Blaine Crabtree!"

"What? I can't suggest it?"

"Are you going to keep asking for it when I'm as big as a house? Or when we have a toddler crying in the next room?"

He smiled and leaned in. "Only one way to find out..."

"CRABTREE! Get your ass over here and finish work unless y'all plan on giving us a show!" A guy yelled from behind us.

Blaine rolled his eyes. "As much as I'd like to show you how much I still find you sexy as hell, I have to get back to work."

I nodded. "Yeah. I guess I understand that."

He leaned in and gave me a quick kiss. "I'll see you soon though, okay? And don't worry about Kristi or any of those other bitches. We do our thing and they do theirs."

"Okay."

With that, he left me standing there while he went back to work. It was hard to see a positive when it seemed liked everything was a big jumbled mess. So instead of trying to find it, I just went back to trying to find normal and got in my car, driving the long, winding road to work.

Chapter 10

It was early. Too early.

But it was the beginning of my second trimester and the morning that I got the call that Beth finally had her baby.

Luxx Ann Marie Watterson was born on March 13th at 5:01 AM...after about twenty-two hours of labor, from what Mom said.

And that scared the hell out of me.

My parents already booked Blaine and I are tickets to fly back to Chicago, and it was a good thing it was a weekend, because Blaine had to basically run home and shower quickly before we hopped on our flight that Friday. He needed to save all the time off he could, so he said. But that meant that I was hardly ever seeing him. Between his work schedule and my school schedule, we would only get a few hours at night and half the time I'd end up falling asleep.

"Did you talk to your sister?" Blaine asked as we finally sat down in the plane. I wasn't sure we were actually going to make our flight on time and had to run down the terminal.

I shook my head. "Not yet. I didn't want to bother her."

He glanced at me out of the corner of his eye. "So she didn't tell you how it was?"

"I don't know if I want to know."

He squeezed my hand. "We still have a few months before that happens and we've at least survived the first trimester."

"Barely," I muttered.

"Meg says that the second trimester is a lot better."

I nodded. "I don't think it could get any worse."

"Come on, Lib. What about going back to positive town? See the good in it. Only twenty-eight more weeks to go and before that we have the wedding and finding our new place."

"That's more like stressors than happy things."

"Okay, what about the fact that you can maybe get a few good naps in while we're there? And by the time we get back, you'll almost be done with school."

"Ugh, between wedding showers, studying for finals, and everything else going on, I don't think I'll have time for anything but quick naps."

"Okay, fine. I give up trying to make you happy then," he threw his arms up in the air, then looked out the window.

I squeezed his knee. "Hey. I'm sorry. It's just... a lot...for both of us."

He turned back to me and put his hand on mine. "I know and I wish there was more I could do to help you out right now, but with my work schedule, I can barely catch up myself."

"Maybe things will slow down once the baby's born."

He laughed. "I don't know about that one."

I THOUGHT MAYBE MOM or Dad would be there to pick us up, so I was literally open-mouthed shocked when I saw my Grandpa Gentry standing at the gate with his wife, Leslie, who was closer to my age than his.

"Grandpa, Leslie, what are you two doing here?" I asked, hugging them both.

Blaine shook both of their hands before Grandpa turned to me, shoving his hands in the pockets of his tweed blazer. "Your Dad had an emergency surgery to do and your mom is up at the hospital, so they asked us to pick you up. I'm sure we weren't the first choice, but they had to take us."

That was probably the case. Dad made it known that he wasn't a fan of Grandpa's former dental assistant and much younger wife with the pixie cut who dressed like a Rockabilly waitress.

Blaine smiled. "Well, it's good to see y'all again."

Grandpa patted his back. "And we hear that you two are getting hitched. Good to have another man in the family, especially one like you."

"Thank you, sir." Blaine nodded.

Leslie put her hand on his shoulder, her red plastic nails practically digging into his skin. "And one with such manners."

"He's only putting on a front now, wait until after we're married," I joked.

Leslie pushed past the boys and stood in front of me. With her red heels she still barely came up to my neck. "Now let's see the ring the boy put on your finger."

I held out my hand and she took it, gaping at the ring. "Oh my! It's gorgeous"

"Thank you."

She looped her arm through mine. "Now, come on, let's get to the car and you can tell me all about your wedding plans on the way to the hospital."

I shrugged as we followed Blaine and Grandpa. "There's not much to tell. It's in June and in Elsbury."

"Louisiana? Your mother didn't tell us that. I knew it was going to be quick and...well...I know about your predicament..." Her eyes lowered to my stomach, then back to me.

I sighed. "Yeah. I guess it moves things a lot quicker, but it'll be nice. I've been going to the church with my Aunt Dee since I moved down there and we both feel comfortable there."

She smiled. "Well, that's what matters, isn't it? A wedding is just one day, but if you don't feel comfortable, it's hell to get through."

I nodded. "Yeah. That's true."

"Now, I know you have your mother and I'm not really your grandmother, but if you do need any help, I'm always here for it. Even if it's just to bend my ear."

I didn't really think it'd be cool to have Aunt Dee's brother-in-law's new wife helping out, but I smiled anyway and said I'd call her if I needed anything. Though, I knew it was an empty promise, at least it was nice that someone wanted to help because that was getting harder and harder to come by.

I HATED HOSPITALS. The last time I was in one, I was hooked up to a bunch of different machines after passing out. I think births were the only happy occasion to be in one, but it still didn't make it any easier.

We walked down the long hallway to the labor and delivery wing and then turned down another hall to where the mothers' rooms were.

There was a giant pink sash on the door that read "It's a girl" and I could hear laughter from inside.

Slowly I opened the door to a room that was bright and much larger than I expected. The whole thing was probably as big as my Aunt Dee's kitchen and living room combined.

Beth sat on a bed leaned against the wall and Brian sat in a chair beside her. On the far wall was my mom with a little pink wrapped bundle in her arms.

I had to choke back tears just looking at the sight. The proud grandma. My little niece. My future baby's cousin.

"Libby, Blaine, you made it!" Brian said and stood up and came over to hug us.

"We wouldn't miss it," I said.

Brian smiled and then hugged Grandpa and Leslie as we all entered the room.

"Hi, Beth, how are you feeling?" I leaned over and kissed my sister on the cheek.

"Honestly? I haven't slept, my boobs hurt, and my lady bits feel like they're on fire. I don't know why in the hell you thought this would be a good idea to do this, too," Beth snapped.

I blinked rapidly. This was not the perky, put-together sister I was used to. She didn't even look the same with her sloppy blonde bun and makeupless face.

Brian swooped in and patted Beth's back. "Now, now. Someone is just a little cranky post-partum. Don't worry, baby, next feeding is soon then you can get a nap in and I'll take Luxxy to the nursery."

Beth just gritted her teeth.

"Do you want to hold her before we have to leave?" Mom asked, her voice quiet.

Usually Mom was always outspoken, so was Dad. It was the quietest she'd ever been.

I nodded and walked over to Mom. "Yeah, that'd be great."

I sat down next to Mom and she handed the little bundle to me, instructing me every step on making sure I watched Luxx's head. "You'll be doing this in a few months, I guess," Mom said, almost muttering.

I looked down at Luxx's little pink face with the big purple bow on her head. Her eyes were closed and she let out a big yawn. I always thought all infants looked the same, but there was something still adorable about them, especially when it was my niece.

"Yeah, we will be," I whispered, staring down at Luxx.

"She's a natural," Leslie piped in. She'll be a great Mommy."

"I guess we owe you two a congrats," Brian said, patting Blaine on the back.

"Ha, yeah, you're stuck with me now," Blaine said and even though I wasn't looking at him, I knew he had that nervous smile on his face.

"Naw, it's not stuck when we like you. Someone has to keep Libby in line."

Blaine laughed. "She does that pretty well on her own."

"Aw, isn't he just the sweetest?" Leslie asked.

"He is," Mom said.

I met my mom's eyes for the first time that day. The way they crinkled at the corners and she had a genuine smile, I knew she meant it. "Thanks, Mom."

She squeezed my hand. "I thought maybe we could grab some lunch with your father and talk wedding plans, then maybe do a little dress shopping before we come back here? That'll give Beth some time to rest."

None of that exactly sounded fun to me. I didn't want to argue with my parents about wedding things or see disapproving looks from my father. I just wanted to sit there all day and hold my little niece in my arms. But with the way Beth looked, I knew she needed a break from people too.

"Yeah. That sounds great, Mom."

SINCE DAD'S OFFICE was downtown, Mom suggested we meet him at a place on Wacker. It was one of those cloth napkin places that served tiny salads and Blaine absolutely hated them. I didn't mind them since I usually preferred not to eat much, but I was starving and was thinking I'd have to make someone drive me through McDonald's later.

We made small talk until my dad rushed into the restaurant. If I thought my sister looked bad, she was practically a beauty queen next to my dad. His normally brown hair was almost fully gray and thinning. He usually always kept his face smooth but now there was almost a full gray beard growing. Some men could pull of the lumber sexual thing, my dad just looked homeless.

"Hey, guys, sorry I'm late, emergency extraction on the point guard for The Bulls. He couldn't wait." Dad hugged me and shook Blaine's hand before taking his seat next to Mom.

"We totally understand," I said, sitting back down.

"Wow." Dad looked at us and smiled. "It's been a crazy couple of months and I think it's going to get even crazier."

"Yep." I nodded, praying things couldn't get any more awkward.

But of course they did.

Dad crossed his arms over his chest, like he always did when he was pissed off and about to lecture. "Now, Libby, your mother tells me that you two want to get married in Elsbury and in only a few months? That sounds awfully quick to me, are you sure you don't want to wait awhile?"

I groaned. "Seriously? I thought we came here to lunch, not to fight about details."

Mom put her hand on Dad's arm. "Honey, we talked about this. Let's not fight about it."

"I'm not fighting, Kathryn. I'm just simply asking them a question." Dad's voice slightly raised with each word, the way it always did when he was mad. It wasn't a question, it was a statement and he wanted answers to that statement.

"With all due respect, Mr. Gentry, and I do respect you, Libby and I did discuss this and we discussed it with Mrs. Gentry," Blaine said.

Dad smirked. "There you go, putting in that Southern charm."

"Jack!" Mom said.

I banged my fist on the table and it shook the glasses, causing everyone to look in my direction. "Okay. Enough. I didn't come here to fight. We flew back here to see my sister and Luxx. If I would have known we would just be fighting, I would have changed our plans and headed back home."

"Libby..." Mom said, reaching her hand out to put it on mine.

"Mom, I love you and Dad. I do. And you know what? It sucks that I got pregnant before Blaine and I were married or I finished school, but it happened and we're moving forward. We love each other, we really do. He wants to help support me as I finish school and we both want to be married before our baby is born."

I sighed and reached down, putting my hand on my stomach as if it would give me some strength. Blaine put his hand on mine and that was what I needed. I didn't realize it at first until I glanced out of the corner of my eye and saw him smiling. That was my positive of the day: that no matter what, he was on my side.

"We want to get married in Elsbury because that's where we both feel comfortable. We don't want anything extravagant and I'm sure it's not what everyone up here wants, but if they can't come, then they can't come. If you don't like it, then you don't have to come either."

Dad laughed but there was no humor in it and then looked at Mom before looking at me. "Well, that was some speech."

"It's also the truth. I know you guys have supported me through everything; hell, I know you're supporting me now by paying for everything, but you sent me to Elsbury to grow up and now I finally am and taking control of things in my life. It may have taken me awhile, but I'd like to think I'm finally getting the hang of things and as long as Blaine stays around, I think I'll be fine."

"I'm not going anywhere," Blaine chimed in.

Mom squeezed my hand. "And neither are we. If you two want to get married in Louisiana, that's fine. We'll all fly there. Just keep us in the loop, okay? We do love both of you and we will continue to support you. Even if sometimes we do some things that may seem unkind."

"Thanks, Mom," I said softly and then looked at my dad.

Dad sighed before finally speaking. "Well, if you two are happy and think you have things figured out, then I'm happy, too. So let's stop fighting and order about fifty main courses because you know they aren't going to give us shit for food."

We all laughed. It may not have been perfect, but at least we were all going to move forward.

At least I hoped we were.

Chapter 11

After lunch, Mom and I dropped Blaine off at the condo and we went shopping. I really wanted to go take a nap like Blaine was probably doing, but if my mom was finally going to get excited about wedding stuff, then I had to go along with it.

"Since we're only three months out, it may be harder for us to find a dress, so I thought maybe we could start while you're here. Of course, we'll have to order a few sizes bigger and you'll probably have to get it tailored," Mom said, her voice drifting as she kept ticking things off her mental list.

"That's fine. I'm sure Aunt Dee could help with any altering."

"Oh and there's invitations. We can order those and you'll have to make sure you get those sent out by early May. I can send you the list we used for Beth's wedding. Some of them may be out dated and everyone probably won't be able to make the trip, but it'll still help you."

"Mom," I interrupted.

She looked at me, but didn't stop walking. The woman could power walk like it was nobody's business.

"Thank you for doing all of this," I said, forcing a smile.

She finally stopped. "Of course. You know I'm always here to help you."

I let out a deep breath. "Yeah, it's all just a little overwhelming."

Mom laughed, putting her arm around me. "I can imagine. School. A baby. Wedding. I don't know how you're doing all of it on your own."

"Well, I'm not completely on my own. Blaine has been helping a bit and I do have some friends in Elsbury as well as Blaine's mom."

"I'm glad you have another support system, even though I wish your father and I could be a bigger part of it."

"Mom, you guys totally are. You've both been financially supporting me through everything. I wouldn't be where I am now if you didn't decide I needed tough love and to move. If it weren't for that, who knows, I'd probably be skipping community college classes and still dating that jerk off Beau."

Mom laughed. "He was kind of a jerk off, wasn't he?"

"Oh the biggest! I definitely got an upgrade."

When we got to the bridal shop, I thought I'd started to relax, until I saw the mannequins and racks of dresses. They were all fitted in beautiful, mermaid-style dresses with lots of detail.

I looked down at my stomach. I wasn't even showing. I felt bloated most days and if I squinted, I swore I could see a slight rounding, but nothing major. I could have still probably fit into some of the form-fitting gowns but for how long? What would my body look like in June?

A middle-aged woman with a tight bun wearing a black pantsuit came to the front of the store. "Hello. Welcome. Do you have an appointment?"

Mom shook her head. "Oh. I'm sorry, I didn't know we needed one. My daughter is just in from Louisiana for the weekend and getting married in a few months, so we thought we'd take advantage of this time and check out some dresses."

The woman pursed her lips and then looked like it was taking everything she had to force a smile. "How lovely. We usually go by appointment only, but I can check in the back and see if anyone is available to see you."

The woman turned on her heel and left us alone at the front of the store.

"Wow, she was real friendly," I muttered.

Mom sighed. "Yes. I can see why you'd rather get married in the south. It seems they have a little bit more hospitality."

"Yeah, I don't think any dress shop would turn us away."

Mom glanced at me out of the corner of her eye. "What do you say we skip the Midwestern rudeness of this dress shop and get some cupcakes, then plan a trip for me to come in and go dress shopping with you in New Orleans?"

I widened my eyes. My mom had never suggested going out for carbs, let alone blowing someone off. "Are you serious?"

She smiled and opened the door. "Serious as a salted caramel cupcake."

AFTER GOING THROUGH a half a dozen cupcakes and two smoothies between the two of us, Mom and I headed back to her and Dad's condo.

I'd grown up in their huge house in an affluent suburb and they'd only lived in their condo in Trump Tower for a few months. The last time I was there, I found it sort of cold and not as inviting, but when we opened the front door and heard Dad and Blaine laughing, I immediately warmed up to the place.

"What's so funny?" Mom asked.

Dad and Blaine were camped out on the leather sectional in the living room with some sports show on the TV, but it didn't even look like they were paying attention to it. They both looked our way when we came in.

Dad pointed at Blaine. "Well, it seems that our future son-in-law has stolen my dog's attention."

I peeked around the corner and saw their French bull dog, Sally, completely passed out on Blaine's lap with her paws in the air and audibly snoring.

"Does this mean you want to take her back with us?" I asked Blaine.

Blaine laughed and shook his head. "As much as I like dogs, I think we should find a place and get used to having a kid around before we add a dog to the mix."

"That seems reasonable," Mom said and took the seat next to Dad.

"Speaking of a place to live, how is the search coming?" Dad asked.

I sighed and plopped down next to Blaine. "Don't ask."

Dad raised an eyebrow. "The market that bad down there?"

I shook my head. "No. Just haven't found anything we've really liked. Everything is too far from either our works or school."

"Are you guys buying or renting?" Dad asked.

"Renting, for now. Someday we'll buy a place, but it's just not in the cards right now," Blaine said.

"Now don't get all pissy with me, Libby, but have you thought about the future past your associates? Are you going to get your bachelor's?" Dad asked, hesitantly.

I opened my mouth to speak, but Blaine put his hand on mine and spoke first. "We've talked about this a lot, sir. I've told her that I can stay home at night with the baby if she wants to take night classes. Her finishing school is a top priority. She came south for some higher education and nothing is going to stop her."

Dad nodded. "That makes me really happy to hear. Kathryn and I have been talking about all of this and though we weren't thrilled at first with everything, we both think that you're doing the best things. You're both more responsible than we ever were at your ages and we want to help you any way we can."

"What your father is saying," Mom interjected, "is that we want to still pay for the rest of your tuition, Libby, and if you do need any help with the down payment of a house, we'll do that for you. Any wedding expense, we have it. You don't have to be afraid of us and what we're going to think. We just want you to know that we support both of you."

I bit my lip to keep my tears at bay. All I'd ever wanted was their acceptance. I wasn't asking for their financial support and even though

I needed it, it meant more to me that they were there to help with anything. "Thank you. Both of you."

Blaine nodded. "We really appreciate it."

"And if I have to travel all the way to Louisiana in the summer for a wedding, then you'd better have a place with air conditioning and some good food," Dad said and laughed.

"Oh! I did find a place online in Elsbury for a reception that looked lovely. The country club in town? It looked like it might have been one of the only places, but I emailed the reservations coordinator while we were at the bakery and she said she might have room for a smaller reception."

I looked at Blaine and he squeezed my hand as if he was urging me to speak my mind. I shouldn't have been angry, but there was something about my hormones that was getting to me. How could she email someplace without even talking to me?

"You do know it is my wedding, right? And Blaine and I have already made plans to have the reception at his parents' place."

Mom's face fell. "Oh."

"We know you're just trying to help, ma'am, but this is kind of a tradition. Both my sisters got married in the Catholic Church and then had their receptions at my parents' place outside. All the women in the family get together and cook a big buffet and everyone can get together and enjoy each other that way," Blaine said, squeezing my hand, which I think he thought might calm me, but instead it was just making me madder.

"No, it's fine. If that's what you two want, then I understand," Mom said.

"It is," I snapped.

"Libby, do you need a chocolate bar or something? You're getting awfully cranky," Blaine said, nudging my side.

"What's that supposed to mean?" I growled.

Blaine put his hands up. "Just saying, if you're hungry I can go get you something."

"You know, Libby, since you want to cook for your wedding, maybe I can help out," Mom said, hesitantly.

I laughed, shaking my head. "Mom, I don't remember the last time you ever cooked."

Dad folded his arms across his chest. "Well, maybe instead of giving your mom so much grief, you could teach her something. Then you'll get food and she can learn to make something that doesn't require a takeout menu."

I raised an eyebrow. "You're not serious."

Blaine patted my back. "I think that sounds like a great idea."

Dad stood up and pulled his phone out. "Just tell me what you need and I'll run to the store and get it."

"This really can't be happening right now," I muttered.

"You can either keep whining or you can help your mom cook, either way, let's get this started," Dad said.

"HAVE THESE THINGS EVER even been used?" I asked, looking at the shiny metal pans.

Mom thought for a moment. "I think you used those when you were here last."

Dad laughed, taking a seat at the breakfast bar. "Now this is something I should record and get on YouTube."

"Stop it, Jack!" Mom swatted him with a dish towel.

"What? I don't remember the last time I've seen you cook and I'm sure your partners at the law firm would be interested too," Dad replied.

Blaine shook his head and took the seat next to Dad. "Now don't make her nervous, Mr. Gentry. You don't want her to mess up and slice her finger or something. Nobody wants blood in their roux."

Dad patted Blaine's back and smiled. "You're probably right. I'll try and be nice."

"Okay, Mom, can you cut up the celery and I'll fry up the garlic and olive oil?"

"This seems like an awful lot of pans for a one pot dish," Mom said, staring at the collection I gathered on the counter.

"At least you have a dishwasher, at Aunt Dee's I have to wash all of these by hand."

Mom widened her eyes. "Oh dear! Jack! We should get that poor woman a dishwasher."

I narrowed my eyes. "I'm sure if she really wanted one, she would have bought it. I think she's doing just fine."

Mom offered a small smile. "Sweetie, but there are three of you living in that house and with all of the cooking she does and with all she's helped us, it would be a nice gesture."

"You know, my ma didn't get a dishwasher until my middle sister moved out and now she loves it," Blaine offered, yelling loud enough probably to try and distract me.

"I'm sure it is a big help with your large family," Mom said, looking back at Blaine.

We cooked in silence because I didn't have anything else to say and I was tired of arguing with her and really just plain tired. Creating life was exhausting.

"I texted Beth and told her we were bringing her up dinner and she said good because she was starving," Mom said.

"I am, too. I'm wondering if this will actually taste as good as it smells," Dad said.

"If you want, I can bring a bowl up to Beth and you guys can eat," I said. I needed to get out. Get some air and away from my parents. It had only been a day with them, but I already needed my space.

"Are you sure you want to do that?" Mom asked.

"Yeah. That's totally fine. I can spend the time with the baby and Beth and then you all can meet me up there."

"Are you sure you're not hungry, too?" Dad asked.

"Yeah, that's fine. I'm sure Blaine and I can grab something on the way back when we get hungry."

"Okay. Fine. I think we can deal with you heading up there before we take over all our precious grand-daughter's time," Dad said.

"You okay if I come with or do you just want sister time?" Blaine asked.

I smiled. "You can come. You probably need the practice in holding a baby."

Blaine laughed. "I have five nieces and nephews. I've done enough snot wiping and holding babies to build up years of experience."

"Well, then I guess you don't need to come," I said with a pout.

Dad tossed Blaine his car keys. "Hey, someone has to drive you."

Blaine stared down at the keys. "Sir, I don't need to drive your car. We can get a cab or something."

"Nonsense. Just take it. It's in spot 19C in the garage."

"Sir, I've never driven anything as fancy as your SUV."

Dad smirked. "Good, then don't wreck it."

IT WAS THE FIRST TIME Blaine had actually driven under the speed limit while I was in the car. He also parked way at the top of the hospital parking garage and so far from other cars that I thought we were going to have to walk a mile just to get in the building.

"Don't you think this is a bit of overkill?" I asked, trudging through the parking lot with the container of gumbo in my hands.

"Hey, your daddy won't kill you and his grand baby, but I don't think he'd have any problem getting rid of me if anything happened to his car."

I rolled my eyes. "You're kind of a drama queen, do you know that?"

He grinned and put his arm around my waist before kissing my forehead. "I learned from the best."

"What's that supposed to mean?" I snapped.

He shook his head and groaned. "Do they give Prozac to pregnant women? You are all over the place and could use some."

"Well excuse me, it's been a long freaking first trimester and I'm trying to grow another life in here."

He squeezed my shoulder. "I know, baby, but you can ease up a bit. Your parents are just trying to help, and the way they know how to, is by throwing money. You can just say 'no thank you' instead of snapping at everybody."

"Why are you being such a jerk?" I tried to hold it in, but tears streamed down my face. I'd always been emotional, but now everything was coming out in big, sobbing gulps.

Blaine stopped in the middle of the parking garage and turned toward me, taking me in his arms and holding me tight. "Shhh, baby. It's okay. There's no reason to cry."

"You think I'm awful!" I sobbed.

He laughed and held me close, running his fingers through my hair. "I never said that."

"But you're thinking it."

"Are you a mind reader?"

I sniffled and shook my head. "No. I just know it. You're working all this overtime and I'm just bitching all the time when I see you. That or falling asleep."

"You need the sleep, I understand it," he said, rubbing my back.

I pulled back and looked up at him, wiping the tears from under my eyes. "Quit making excuses for me, I know I'm awful."

His eyes met mine. "Baby, you're not awful, okay? I don't know what to say to make you feel better, but just know that everything going on around us is crazy. It's going to keep getting crazier and you've been going with the flow so much, I had a feeling you'd snap soon."

"I didn't expect it to be while we were here and over something so stupid."

He laughed. "I think Alicia hit Ronnie in the head with the remote control when she was in labor with Callie. Every pregnant woman goes a little crazy, us menfolk just have to figure out how to live with it."

I sniffled. "I promise to try and not to hit you with the remote. Try being the keyword."

He shook his head and smiled. "I'm sure you'll try but probably not succeed and I'm sure you'll have more breakdowns, but we'll just have to power through them."

I sighed. "Yeah. Hopefully we can survive them."

He put his arm around my shoulder and pulled me next to him as we continued to walk through the parking garage. "You know, Meemaw used to say that everything we experience, all of our ups and downs, is the trail of our life. Sometimes it veers one way and sometimes it veers the other. You get some mangled roots and fallen branches, but it keeps going."

I shook my head and laughed. "I'm not even sure I know what that means."

He squeezed my shoulder. "I think it means that just because we have a few bad days, doesn't mean that the worlds going to end and we'll get through it."

I smiled. "I guess you're right."

He leaned in and kissed me lightly. "I know I am."

BEFORE WE EVEN GOT to Beth's room, I could hear a baby crying and then Beth's frantic voice, "She just won't stop crying! I don't know what to do!"

"Maybe this is a bad time..." Blaine said as we approached the door.

"When was the last time she was fed and changed?" A calm voice asked.

"She just fucking ate! All she does is scream, sleep, shit, and latch onto my tits until she does one of the other three again!"

"Ma'am. That's what babies do. She's just a newborn. It'll get easier," the voice said again.

I took a chance at glancing in the room and Brian caught my eye. "LIBBY! You're here! Hey, Beth, your sister and Blaine are here with dinner. Isn't that great?"

Brian opened the door with his eyes wide as if he was asking for us to help him in any way we could.

Even though Brian was always a huge goober with his balding head and jogging suits, he was always put together. This was the most disheveled I'd ever seen him with his scruffy face and faded t-shirt with wrinkled jeans.

I would have rather run in the other direction, than walked into the room, but something pulled me forward. Maybe it was my motherly instinct, or maybe I just wanted to see if this was what it was really like to give birth.

"Yes. We're here and we brought some gumbo that Mom and I made," I said, sheepishly entering the room with Blaine in tow.

Beth was sitting on the bed with her hair all over the place and her makeup running. A nurse was standing next to her with a bundled, crying Luxx in her arms.

"Do you want me to try taking her?" Blaine asked.

The nurse looked at Beth and Beth waved her arms. "Yeah, whatever. See if you can do something about her."

Blaine took the little bundled baby in his arms and set her down in the wheeled cart where a makeshift bed was made. "Hey, Brian, why don't we try taking her for a walk down the halls? That used to help my oldest niece."

Brian audibly sighed with relief. "Yeah. That sounds great."

"Let me know if you need anything else, Mrs. Watterson," the nurse said and followed the boys out of the room.

I was alone with my sister. Usually I would have loved spending time with her, but with her being so out of character and moody, I wasn't sure. Two hormonal women in one room probably wasn't a good thing.

"Um, Mom and I made this for you. It actually seems edible," I said, setting the container down on the tray by her bed.

Beth glared at me. "I wish someone would have told me that motherhood fucking sucks."

I sat down in the chair next to her. "I'm sure it's not that bad. It hasn't even been twenty-four hours."

She shook her head. "I really thought I could handle everything. I'm a teacher for crying out loud. But you do all this work to carry them for nine months, then have the painful experience of pushing an eight pound human out of your vagina and having it torn in half. THEN after all that, they just want to latch onto your nipple and scream or poop when they aren't attached. I didn't think this was how it was going to be at all."

"Wow. That makes me really excited to follow in your footsteps," I muttered.

She sighed. "Sorry. I shouldn't be telling you all of this, but no one told me and I feel like I was really unprepared for this whole mess."

"Well, at least you have Brian's help and his parents and Mom and Dad."

"Pft. Yeah, but he can't get up with her in the middle of the night to breast feed."

"Then why don't you just do formula or pump something so he can take a feeding if it's that hard?" I asked.

She shook her head. "The doctor said my milk may have not fully come in and it'll get easier as we both learn. I want to do this. I don't want to fail and I feel like I keep failing over and over again."

I put my hand on hers as the tears streamed down her face. "Hey. You're not failing. You brought life into this world and obviously she's doing great since she has one hell of a set of lungs on her."

Beth laughed and then sniffled. "I can't believe you're going to be doing this too in a few months. I would say congratulations, but right now I'm not sure if that's the best thing to say."

"It is. I'm happy, I really am. And we're going to have to figure out a way to get Luxx down the aisle with Blaine's nieces as one of my flower girls since Luxx's mama will be standing at my side as the matron of honor."

Beth smiled. "You still want me as your matron of honor, even though I've just bitched you out?"

"Of course I do. You're my sister. Even if you're complaining, you're just looking out for my best interest."

She laughed. "I try. Even though I'm not sure that I want to go to Louisiana when it's going to be hotter than hell in June."

"I'll make sure everyone gets hand fans like true Southern belles," I said.

"You'd better."

WHEN BLAINE AND I LEFT the hospital, I got a text from Kristi that she wanted Blaine and I to stop by her place the next day. Our flight wasn't until Sunday, but I wanted to spend as much time with my sister as possible. I think she needed it, especially since Luxx seemed to really like Blaine. Or she just liked the fact that he pushed her around in her little baby cart.

I don't know. We've been really busy and only have another day.

Kristi was quick to reply.

Please? Just for a few minutes.

I reluctantly agreed and Blaine and I drove over to her and Gabe's apartment in Wrigleyville.

"Baby, we don't have to do this. I can text Kristi and tell her that something happened with your sister and we can't make brunch."

I shook my head and got out of the car, peering up at their brownstone. "No. We should do this. Get it over with."

Blaine came around to my side of the car and took my hand. "Just say the word and I'll come up with an escape plan if we need it."

"Thanks. I hope we don't."

We walked up the cobblestone path until we were at the red door of their unit. I rang the doorbell and heard voices behind it that quickly silenced on the second ring. I thought Gabe would be out for his morning basketball league and was just expecting to leave with Kristi for brunch.

But when Kristi opened the door, she wasn't alone and the room was full of my sorority sisters, streamers, balloons, and everything in baby decor.

"Surprise!" everyone yelled.

I widened my eyes and stepped inside, looking around Kristi's small living room that had been transformed with different stuffed animals on every surface someone wasn't sitting on and a huge cake on the coffee table that read, "Congratulations Libby"

"What's all this?" I asked.

Kristi took me by the arm and pulled me into the apartment. "I wanted to make up for being such a bitch in New Orleans and I also wanted to throw you a baby and wedding shower before you left. It's kind of last minute but I hope you don't mind."

I felt the tears welling up in my eyes. "No. It's perfect. You didn't have to do any of this."

She squeezed my arm. "Yes. I did. That's what sisters are for."

A few minutes stop turned into a few hours with Blaine and I opening gift after gift of either kitchen appliances or gender neutral baby clothes and toys. Everyone was more than generous and I was starting to think of how much it was going to be to ship all of it home when it barely fit into my dad's SUV.

As Blaine loaded the last gift in the back, Kristi pulled me into a hug. "I'm so sorry I was such a bitch, Libby. I know a bunch of gifts won't make up for that, but I hope you can forgive me."

I let go of her and smiled. "Of course, Kristi. What are sisters and bridesmaids for?"

Chapter 12

Our trip to Chicago was a whirlwind and so was life back in Elsbury.

By the time my fourth month of pregnancy was approaching, my belly was starting to round and it was getting harder to wear my jeans without leaving them unbuttoned. People would constantly stare at my stomach when I was at school or working and wait for me to tell them that I wasn't just getting fat.

This also didn't help the fact that we didn't tell the priest we were expecting and now we had two weekends back-to-back of all day marriage classes.

I didn't really understand why we needed to go to classes, but it was what we had to do to get married in the church. So I rubberbanded my jeans closed, put on this biggest, flowiest top I could find and headed out with Blaine early on Saturday morning.

The church in Elsbury only had a few weddings over the summer so they combined with churches from four different towns to hold marriage classes in the town hall in Caimon, which was about twenty miles from Elsbury and in swamp country.

"Ready for one hell of a long day?" Blaine asked as we pulled into the parking lot.

I blew out a breath. "Yeah. What are we even supposed to be doing?"

Blaine looked at his phone and scrolled through a few things. "Ah, here it is. Nine to five with a break for lunch, St. Patrick's Church hall in Caimon, and..."

"And what?"

He put his phone down and his eyes met mine. "We're going to be talking about Christian sexuality."

"I beg your pardon?"

He laughed, shaking his head as he shoved his phone into his pocket. "Obviously we don't need knowledge of any of that."

"So...is this a 'don't have sex' seminar or something porny?"

Blaine laughed even harder as he opened his door and got out before circling the car to open my door. "I'm going to go with the first one."

I jumped out of the car and smiled. "Well, we definitely don't need that. Let's just hope it goes by quickly."

He put his arm around me, guiding me down the brick path to the double doors of the building. "We can only hope."

A guy with a military-style hair cut dressed in a polo and khakis opened the door for us. "Is that Blaine Crabtree?"

I stared at Blaine as he smiled at the guy. "Yes it is, and don't hate me, but I'm not recalling your name."

The guy shook Blaine's hand briskly. "Eli Chardon, I played second base for Caimon."

Blaine's eyes lit up. "Oh, hey, man. I didn't recognize you without the shaggy hair or me striking you out."

Eli patted Blaine's back as he let go of his hand. "Yeah, yeah. We all know you were the best at the game."

"Yeah, high school has been a few years though. I'm a little rusty."

Eli's green eyes caught mine and he nodded in my direction. "And don't tell me that you've been ditching baseball to spend time with this little lady. Is the school legend getting hitched?"

"Yep. This is my fiancée, Libby. She's from Chicago."

Eli shook my hand. "Damn glad to meet you, Libby. Wow. I can't believe we're both here."

"Are you getting hitched too?" Blaine asked as he followed him up the stairs to a large room with horrible fluorescent lighting and paneled walls. There were rows of folding tables with two folding chairs behind each one, set facing a standing white board.

Eli nodded. "Yeah, my girl didn't want to wait and since I'm bound to get deployed here soon, we decided it was best not to." He pointed at a girl with long, brown hair, standing in a circle with a pair of couples. "That's Mandy over there. She was on the spirit squad at Caimon. Hey, Mandy! Come see who is getting hitched!"

This was the last thing I wanted to do. I wasn't there to make new friends or rekindle old friendships that Blaine had. I just wanted to sit, do our thing, and leave. But the petite brunette walked over to us and Eli put his arm around her. "Mandy, I don't know if you remember, but Blaine Crabtree was the star pitcher at Elsbury and this is his fiancée, Libby. She's a Yankee, but you can still like her."

Mandy limply shook both of our hands. "It's nice to meet you both."

God things were awkward. I needed an out. That's when I spotted the table of pastries and orange juice. "Excuse me, I'm just going to go grab something to eat before we start."

"I'll get something with you and let the boys chat before we start," Mandy said.

Awesome. More random small talk that I didn't want, but I grinned and followed her over to the table anyway.

Truth be told, I was starting to crave more salts than sweets and the donuts and cherry covered items didn't look that appealing to me, but I still put a bear claw on my plate so I'd have something to do.

"So, when are you due?" Mandy asked.

I blinked hard and dropped my donut on the floor.

"Oh my goodness, I'm sorry!" Mandy said and picked it up.

"No, it's fine," I said and threw away the donut in the trash and picked up another one, putting it on my plate.

"I'm sorry. I-I-I shouldn't have asked."

I shook my head. "No. It's fine. I just...I didn't think this was the place to tell people. How did you know?"

She looked behind us at Eli then looked at me, nodding toward my stomach. "That shirt isn't really hiding much and you look like I did when we had Brenden."

I cocked an eyebrow. "You have a son? Eli didn't mention that."

She pursed her lips. "Yeah, this really isn't the place to talk about that. A Christian sexuality class for the heathens. I had him our senior year of high school and now that Eli's finally enlisted we figured we should get it over with and tie the knot, so Brenden and I could get the military benefits."

"Wow. Yeah, it sounds like that'll be a good thing."

Mandy laughed nervously. "Sorry I made things more awkward, but if you do need to talk about anything or you need baby stuff, I still have a ton."

I forced a smile. I wasn't sure what to think of her yet, but my first thought was that I kind of liked her. "Thanks. I appreciate it."

"Oh, looks like Mr. Costeu is here. I think he enjoys talking about sex and Catholics too much," Mandy said, nodding toward the doorway as an older man walked in. He was sporting a long, gray ponytail and a goatee like some hippie Jesus.

Mandy scooted off to Eli and they took a seat at one of the tables. I followed her lead and sat down next to Blaine at the table next to theirs.

"So this old dude is going to talk to us about sex?" Blaine whispered.

"I guess so," I muttered.

Mr. Costeu walked to the front of the room and wrote his name on the white board. "Hello, everybody, I'm Mr. Costeu. Some of you may recognize me from the congregation, here, in Caimon and wonder why the hell the guy with seven kids is here to talk to you about Christians and sexuality."

His accent was very thick and he projected his words out to all of us. No one knew if they should laugh so everyone just kind of stared at him.

He clasped his hands together. "Today we are going to talk about how Christian marriage plays into sexuality and family planning. Sex and children are an integral part of married life. This program explains and explores the traditional Christian vision of how God's plan for marriage includes an approach to sex that is honest, faithful, and open to life."

Without even thinking about it, I rubbed my stomach. Like somehow he was talking to me directly and knew that Blaine and I were going to be raising a child soon.

"This day will consist of presentations about the nature of human sexuality, its right use in the context of Christian marriage, an introduction to modern methods of Natural Family Planning — highly effective, healthy, marriage-building, and morally sound ways of planning a family — as well as couple discussion and a question-and-answer period."

And that was where my thoughts of this class being for us ended. We didn't exactly need the Natural Family Planning method. We sort of had that part figured out.

"Now, before we begin, I want you to all do me a favor and instead of looking at me, face your partner," Mr. Costeu said.

I shifted in my chair, turning toward Blaine, biting at my bottom lip. This was one of the most uncomfortable situations I'd ever been in and I felt like I'd either throw up or pass out from embarrassment.

"Now, grab your partner's hands, look into their eye and repeat after me."

I did as he said and looked at Blaine, trying to block out the awkwardness.

"Now, repeat after me, 'I love you. I'm committed to you and to our future in a Christian marriage and to raise our children with the teachings of Jesus Christ, our Lord and Savior.'"

Everyone repeated after him, but the words got caught in my throat and I found myself just staring at Blaine. Then he opened his mouth and his soft words came through. "I love you. I'm committed to you and our future in a Christian marriage and to raise our child in the teachings of Jesus Christ."

We may have just been repeating what the guy said, but when his eyes were on mine and the way he squeezed my hand, I knew it meant more to him. I knew that even though our situation wasn't ideal, we were going to do it, together. We had the support of everyone around us and just because we didn't do it in the order of marriage then baby, didn't mean anything was different. We still loved each other. We were still going to get married and raise a baby.

And maybe that's what we were supposed to get out of the whole day.

GETTING READY FOR A baby, a wedding, and trying to find a new place was a lot more work than I thought it would be.

"Did you email me your part of the list?" I asked, sitting on Blaine's bed and resting my head against the pillows while he sat at the end of it, a controller in his hand as he played some sort of war video game.

"Uh, maybe."

I rolled my eyes. "Seriously, we have to order these invitations, address them, and get them out by the beginning of May."

"Yeah and it's still only March."

I groaned. "Blaine!"

He paused the game and looked over at me. "Why don't you go downstairs and ask my mama for it? I'm sure she'll be more help than I am."

I scooted down toward the end of the bed. "Blaine, don't you think we should try and start doing some more on our own? We're having a baby. We're getting married. All of this in only a few months and we both haven't even lived on our own."

He smiled. "Which is why I think we should still have my mama do stuff for us while we can."

I rolled my eyes and stood up. "Fine, I'll go ask her."

"And see if she can make us some snacks while you're down there!" he yelled as I opened the door and headed down the stairs.

I expected to see Vicki in the kitchen, but when she wasn't there or the living room, I headed out to the front porch. It was my first Louisiana spring and it didn't disappoint with the warm sunshine and cool breeze that slightly rocked the porch swing.

Vicki was bent over in the front, a small shovel in her hand as she stabbed at the garden bed.

I walked down the small, wooden porch steps. "Um, hey, Vicki?"

She gasped and put her hand over her heart and sat up. "Oh, Libby, honey, you should never scare a woman with a trowel."

I winced. "Sorry."

She shook her head. "No problem at all. What can I help you with, dear?"

I bit my bottom lip and made a circle with my foot on the step. I don't know why it bothered me to ask her for things; maybe it was because I never really had to ask anyone for much. I'd always just got what I wanted, whether it was money from my parents or something new for my car. It wasn't until I moved to Louisiana that I had to actually work for things and asking for help was a whole new game.

"Well, I've been asking Blaine to help with his half of the wedding guest list so we can order invitations and he's been kind of procrastinating on it, so he thought I should ask you."

She smiled, pushing her blonde hair out of her eyes. "You should have asked me in the first place, honey. You know a man wouldn't be able to keep track of that."

She stood up and slowly walked past me toward the house. "Come on inside with me. I think I still have everything from Alicia's wedding."

I followed her into the house and down the small hallway until we were in a room that was painted bright yellow and filled with toys. The only thing adult about it was a small, white desk with a recipe box on the shelving unit above it.

Vicki opened the box and scanned through it before handing it to me. "Most of these names should be up to date in here."

I looked at the contents and saw dozens of little note cards with Vicki's cursive scrawl across each one. "Thank you. This helps a lot."

"Are y'all planning on having a lot of people coming in from your side?"

I shrugged. "I don't think so. We want to keep it under 150 invites. Is that going to be too much for you to cook for?"

She laughed. "Honey, I think there were about four-hundred people at Meg's wedding and I didn't have your Aunt Dee's help. It was just me and Alicia and Meemaw, cooking all day down at the church and bringing tray after tray down to the country club. I swore when Billy's mama finally showed up at the reception and THEN asked if there was anything she could do to help, I wanted to pour the last of the gumbo all over her frilly dress."

"Oh geez, I hope you didn't!"

She shook her head. "No. I wouldn't do that. Though I've thought about it more than once."

I chewed at my bottom lip. "You know my mom isn't much of a cook and my sister just had a baby, so I'm not sure how much help they'll be."

Vicki smiled and put her arm around me. "I've already talked to your mom quite a few times. She emailed me not long after you and Blaine announced the baby and your nuptials. At first it was both of us kind of commiserating together, but then we both knew that you two were meant to be together. She knows that she has her talents and I have mine and we'll work together to make them happen."

I raised my eyebrows. I had no idea the two even talked.

Vicki squeezed my shoulder. "Now you'd better run along and get those in your computer or do whatever you need to do to order those invitations. Meemaw's been asking for hers just about every day and you don't want to see Meemaw when she's ornery."

I had never seen Meemaw without a scowl on her face but I smiled anyway. "Thanks, Vicki. I'll do that."

Chapter 13

After finally ordering, addressing, and mailing all of our wedding invitations it was time to get on with the next step of pre-weddingness: registering.

We still hadn't found a place, so I had no idea where we'd even put the stuff, but we planned on going on another house hunt after we were done hitting the department stores in the city.

"What the hell is this?" Blaine asked, holding up some sort of a silver utensil.

I stared at the list that the lady at the registration desk gave us. I didn't see anything on there that I wasn't sure of what it was and I was pretty sure the silver thing wasn't on the "must have bridal registry" list. "I don't know and if we don't know what it is, then we don't need it."

"What we need is a new gaming system. How am I supposed to teach our baby all about medieval gaming and sports if we don't have a new system?"

I rubbed my stomach, which was now definitely pooching out. It didn't look like I was full-on pregnant, but that I had at least smuggled a small loaf of bread under my shirt. "We don't even know if it's a he or she yet, so how do you know if our baby girl will like video games?"

Blaine smiled and kneeled down in front of my stomach and tickled it. "Two more weeks and we'll find out if we have the big P or the little P."

I squirmed and giggled. "Stop it! We're in public."

"What? Everybody's got a P."

"Do you really need to call it that?" I asked.

He shrugged. "What would you prefer that I call it?"

I swatted his arm and started walking down the aisle. "I don't know, but not that."

Blaine followed me down the aisle toward the bed linens. "Do we really need all of these things? Isn't my comforter good enough?"

I wrinkled my nose. "Your comforter always smells like sweat and grass."

"Yeah, it's called 'Eau de Blaine' and you love it."

I laughed. "I'm not sure about that."

"Are you going to spray all your girly shit over our bedding and make me get something pink?"

I frowned. "Did you seriously just say that to me?"

"What? It's an honest question."

I glared at him. "No, I won't be getting a pink comforter but if you don't want anything that smells like me, maybe we don't need to be sleeping or living together."

Okay, it was a stupid reason to get all pissy, but it still bothered me. I'd been working so long just to get him to agree to move in together, and before that he'd had so many more commitment issues. Now that things were finally going smoothly, every time there was a little bump it always threw me off and upset me.

Blaine put his hands on my shoulder. "Hey, baby, don't be like that."

"Well, you don't need to say those things."

He pulled me in for a hug. "I'm sorry. I won't make fun of your girly shit anymore when you're all crazy hormonal."

I swatted his chest. "No, you won't make fun of it ever if you want to keep me and Libby junior around."

He kissed my forehead before pulling back and grabbing the registry scanner from me. "It's Blaine junior and this camouflage bedroom set is calling to him. He told me, telepathically, from your stomach."

I leaned and kissed Blaine on the lips before taking the registry gun back and heading in the opposite direction of camouflage. I also made a mental note to check the registry and probably take off half of what he scanned when he thought I wasn't looking.

After registering my feet ached, but Blaine really wanted to check out one more place.

"I think this could be the one, baby. It's a little farther out than we wanted to be, but it's real nice."

I thought we'd be heading back toward Elsbury, but Blaine got off at four exits before we normally would.

"Where are we going?" I asked, peering out the window.

"This place is actually still in New Orleans."

I raised an eyebrow. "Won't that be far for you since your work is usually in a different parish?"

He shook his head. "Naw, it won't be too far of a commute for me and it'll be a lot closer for you to go to school."

"Um, I don't know if you noticed but this isn't anywhere near St. Joseph."

He smiled and glanced at me out of the corner of his eye. "I'm not talking about community college, I'm talking about after. When you're ready to finish your degree."

I blinked. We'd talked about me finishing my degree before, but I really thought it would be a ways off. I did plan on finishing my associates at some point after the baby was born, but I wasn't in a hurry. "Really?"

He put his hand on my knee and squeezed it. "Yes, really. You moved back here for me and I convinced you to go to school here, so I have to keep to my promise and you have to finish school. If you need to take night classes or we need to work with my mama on taking some time off to watch him while you have classes, then we'll do it."

I wiped a fallen tear from my cheek and leaned over, placing a quick kiss on Blaine's cheek. "Thank you," I whispered.

"You don't need to thank me, baby. For you, I'd do anything."

WE TURNED DOWN A STREET that was lined with boutique shops and small cafes. There were people walking down the cobblestone paths, looking in windows, and genuinely looking happy.

I expected us to turn down another street into some residential area, but instead Blaine slowed down and pulled into a spot in front of a mint green building.

"Is the neighborhood around the corner from here or something? Is that why we're parking here? I don't know if I'm going to like having to lug groceries and a baby a few blocks." I looked out the window, trying to see any hint of a subdivision.

Blaine shook his head and pointed out the front window. "No, baby, we're here."

I looked out at the mint green building with the two bright yellow doors and red shutters. This couldn't be it. It looked more like an artist haven than someplace I could see us living.

"That place?" I asked.

He nodded and opened the door, coming around to my side and helping me out. "Yeah, Don told me about it. One of his friends lives here now but is graduating in May so we'd be able to have it when he moves out, right after the wedding. It's a shotgun style duplex, so we'd have one side wall neighbor, but that ain't too bad. It's better than living with my parents."

"That's very true." I smiled and let him lead me to the front porch.

It didn't look like my dream place. I always used to think that I wanted to live in the city, in a condo like my parents. But the more time I spent at Aunt Dee's or Blaine's the more I realized that I liked the quiet and openness of the country.

Blaine knocked on the front door and nothing happened. He knocked again. Still nothing. He then pounded his fist on the door and finally we heard some shuffling. Then a guy with short black dreads, wearing nothing but a pair of blue basketball shorts answered.

"Hi, I'm Blaine, Don sent me over to look at the place."

The guy smiled widely. "Oh, yeah! Sorry I forgot about y'all coming. Come on in, look around," he said and took a step back.

We walked into a small living room with light wood laminate floors and pale yellow walls. The room may have looked even smaller because the narrow space was crammed with a big, plaid couch and a fifty inch TV as well as various clothes and pizza boxes piled up.

"Sorry about the mess, man. It's finals week," the guy said, picking up some clothes and setting them on the couch.

"It's fine. Don't worry about it," Blaine said.

The living room led to a kitchen with a white island being the only thing that separated it from the living room. A few steps later and we were in a small hallway with a white subway tiled bathroom on one side and a bedroom that was crammed with furniture on the other. The hallway ended with a decent sized bedroom that had French doors on the opposite side that were open, letting in the spring breeze from a small courtyard.

"Oh, man, this is nice. We could sit out here and watch the sunset, maybe have the baby in a little swing. I can just picture us here now. I can even see that other room being the baby's and getting a crib and changing table in there. We could even put a desk in so if you need to stay up late and do homework and if the baby's fussing for you to hold him, you can do both," Blaine said.

I couldn't see any of that in my head, especially not doing homework while holding a baby. But the way Blaine's eyes lit up, it was the first time that I'd seen him so excited about anything baby or wedding related.

So I smiled. "Yeah. I think this may be the one."

"Really?" He raised his eyebrows.

I nodded. "I think this could work out for us."

I was lying through my teeth, but if he could put himself through everything for me, then I knew I could do the same for him. And maybe the place wouldn't be as bad as I thought it was. I learned to love living in Louisiana when I thought I'd hate it, so this place wouldn't be any different. And hopefully it would be temporary. Hopefully.

The guy grinned. "All right, that's dope, y'all. Let me just call the landlord and give him y'alls information."

"Sound great," Blaine said as the guy pulled out his phone.

Blaine leaned in, pressing his forehead to mine. "You sure you're okay with this place? I know it isn't ideal, but..."

I stopped his words and placed a small kiss on his lips. "It's perfect. This is going to be our new home."

He held my hands and squeezed them. "Yeah. It is."

Chapter 14

I had never waited so long for something as I did for my next ultrasound.

I guess it did help that I was also studying for finals, mailing out wedding invitations, and packing.

I was still refusing to buy maternity clothes, not that there was anything wrong with them, there was just something about still being able to fit into my normal clothes that made me feel better. Even though I happened to be wearing cropped yoga pants and an oversized LSU t-shirt that was actually Britt's.

Since the weather was getting hotter, Blaine started work really early in the morning and was able to get off in the afternoon. I was trying to do the same thing on days I worked, even though it was getting harder and harder to stay awake all day and I found myself napping by three every day.

But not that day.

Blaine rolled up to Aunt Dee's house at two and picked me up to drive to the doctor's office and find out the gender of our baby. This time I didn't have to go and hunt him down.

"Is that your shirt?" Blaine asked as I got into the car.

I shook my head. "No, it's Britt's, but does it matter?"

He shrugged as he pulled out of the driveway. "No, just hadn't seen that on you before. I thought you'd already be on Magazine Street looking for some maternity boutiques and dressing better than any pregnant woman in town."

I smirked. "If I felt like wasting my money on clothes that I was only going to wear another five months."

Blaine stared at me then back at the road then looked at me again. "Who are you and what have you done with my Libby?"

"What? I really don't see the point in buying new things when I'm only going to wear them a few months."

That, and I really did have a problem with buying such a bigger size. I didn't want to think about what size my maternity clothes would be or how my body was going to change after having a baby. My counselor said to try and see the positive side, but when I kept looking at my rounded belly, I wasn't seeing a life being created, I was just seeing the bacon pizza I'd wolfed down the night before because I was craving it.

He smiled. "Well, if you really feel that way, it's fine, but you can still go and buy new clothes. It's not like we're poor."

I leaned in and kissed his cheek. "I appreciate your concern, but I'd much rather find a new Pottery Barn bed than buy myself a new wardrobe."

He grinned. "Now there's the girl I know."

THIS TIME BLAINE DIDN'T try to find magazines to read and instead played a game on his phone while we waited for my name to be called back.

The same ultrasound woman we had before came to the door and called my name. I thought I'd be a little less nervous this time, but I constantly felt flutters in my stomach. I'd started to feel them a lot lately. It was as if there were little butterflies in my stomach, all the time.

We got into the ultrasound room and I hopped up on the chair while Blaine sat in the stool next to me.

"Are we getting a lot of movement from baby?" the woman asked as she pulled up a seat to the work station.

"Um..." I bit my bottom lip. Should I have been? Was it a bad sign?

"Any kicks? Rolls?"

I shook my head. "No..."

The woman's face fell but then she quickly turned her lips up again. "What about anything like flutters? Like there are butterflies flying around in your stomach?"

Did the woman read my mind? "Uh, yeah, I've had a lot of that, but I think it's just nerves."

She smiled. "That sounds more like your little baby is very active if you're having a lot of that."

I let out a deep breath that I didn't realize I was holding in and leaned back as I lifted up my shirt.

"Now just like last time, I'm going to tuck this paper towel into your pants here and put some warm gel on your stomach. Now do you two want to know what you're having or want it to be a surprise?"

"We want to know," Blaine said before I could even open my mouth.

The woman laughed. "Someone is anxious. Hoping for a little sports watching buddy?"

"I don't want to jinx it, but yes ma'am, I am."

She laughed again and pressed the wand to my stomach. As soon as she pressed it down, my stomach turned and it felt like I had a giant rolling pin that was making the rounds of my stomach.

"Wow, for someone who says they haven't felt many kicks, this baby sure is moving," the woman said.

She turned the screen toward us and I couldn't take my eyes off of it. Last time it just looked like a little bean, but this time the baby had transformed. It now looked like an actual human. Well, a very tiny one.

I could make out the head and tiny arms and legs that would not stop kicking. The woman kept moving the wand and with each movement, I'd watch as the little baby rolled on the screen.

"Wow, we may have a swimmer. Better call Coach Cal now and see if we can already get em' on the swim team, " Blaine said.

The woman moved the wand down closer to my pelvis. "And it looks like we'll have the new all parish swimmer for the boy's team. Congrats you two, it's a boy!"

Blaine stared at the screen wide eyed and then pointed at it. "Is that his?"

I looked where Blaine was pointing and sure enough, there was a pretty sizeable member between his legs. There was no denying his gender.

The woman laughed. "Yes. That would be his penis."

"Man, he really is my boy!"

I smacked Blaine's stomach and that just made him laugh.

"I'm just kidding, baby." He kissed my forehead.

I looked at the screen, then up at Blaine. "He's ours isn't he? This is real. We're really going to have a little boy, aren't we?"

He grinned and kissed me again. "Yeah, baby, we sure are."

Chapter 15

Finals were only a week away and then right after my mom was coming in to go dress shopping.

I wasn't looking forward to either.

"Okay, time is up for politics, now onto math," Sawyer said, closing his book. We decided to do a system of spending a half an hour on each subject before moving to the next.

"Math, my favorite."

I grabbed my math book from the counter. We decided to spend the day studying at Aunt Dee's since Britt had a softball game so her and Aunt Dee were gone all day.

"Are you sure you can handle all of this right now, darlin'?" Sawyer raised an eyebrow.

I let out a deep breath, my stomach falling over my yoga pants. The farther along I got, the bigger and harder my stomach got. And ever since the ultrasound, our little boy decided he was going to let me know he was there and move as much as he could. "I have to be, don't I? Summer classes start a week after finals, then the wedding, then moving, and another set of finals before the baby comes. Maybe I'll get a break sometime in August."

"Honey, you are going to wear yourself thin and that's not good for you or the baby. You need to try and slow it down."

"Seriously, Sawyer, there is no time. I just have to make sure I prioritize things and get it done."

He sighed. "Okay, just let me know if you need anything. You know I'm always here to help."

"Can you go dress shopping with my mom?"

He laughed. "I mean, I probably would look good in white, but I think your mom might notice."

I groaned. "Yeah, she'll notice you aren't pregnant."

"Or a girl."

"That too."

Sawyer shook his head. "Just take it one day at a time. One hour. One minute. One second. Focus on one thing and then move to the next."

"Easier said than done," I muttered.

"Well, then we'd better put it into action. Let's start with algebra, then we can talk dresses."

FIVE FINALS. THREE on the same day. I thought I was going to collapse from exhaustion by the time my last final ended on Thursday.

I'd already had my caffeine intake for the day, but I was seriously thinking about grabbing an espresso or Diet Coke before I headed back home.

But as I headed for my car, there was a beautiful blond man leaning against it. My beautiful blond man.

"Hey, Libby," Blaine's eyes lit up and he pushed off the car as I approached.

"What are you doing here? I thought you had work?"

He smiled and gave me a big hug. "I did. The job was down the road from here and we finished up early. You've been running on empty for a while, so I thought we could do something to celebrate the end of your finals."

I raised an eyebrow. "Are you serious right now? You know my mom is coming in tomorrow, I have work, and still a ton more stuff to do."

He leaned back and put his hands on my shoulders. "Trust me, okay? Take some time for yourself and for me before it's more than just the two of us around."

I sighed. "Okay, Blaine. You win. Where are we going?"

He shook his head and then opened the door to his car that was parked next to mine. "You'll see."

I smirked. "Okay. Hopefully you aren't wanting to try sex in the back of this thing because I'm not as limber as I was in February."

He laughed, shaking his head. "Wouldn't dream of it, unless of course you wanted to."

I got in and closed the door behind me, then leaned in and kissed his cheek as he got in. "You can dream all you want. It's not happening."

WE DROVE DOWN THE MAIN road until Blaine pulled into a strip mall not far from campus. It had a Chinese restaurant and a coffee shop that Sawyer and I would frequent a lot since the boy had an addiction to Americanos.

"Um, I'm really not in the mood for coffee and I've already had enough today," I said, staring out the window.

Blaine shook his head. "Naw, I've got something else in mind."

He stepped out of the car and went around to my side, opening the door for me. Just as my feet hit the pavement, a truck door opened across from us and out came Nikki.

"Hey, y'all made it!" She came bounding over to us with her way-too-perky boobs practically flying out of her tank top.

I was told that my boobs were supposed to get bigger with pregnancy and I was still barely filling a B cup. It wasn't fair.

"Yep we did," Blaine said, putting his arm around me.

"Um, this isn't a plan to do something weird is it?" I asked, looking between the two of them.

Nikki laughed. "Depends on your definition of weird."

I shrugged. "I don't know. Hunting. Mudding. Orgy."

Blaine and Nikki both laughed hard and when they finally caught their breath, Blaine shook his head and squeezed my shoulder. "No, baby. No outdoor activities or sex. Just something relaxing. Nikki told me this was a good place to go for it."

"What is?" I cocked an eyebrow as Blaine led me around the truck and down the sidewalk. He stopped in front of a building that was literally just around the corner from the coffee shop.

I looked up at the small, purple sign that read 'House of Nails'. "We are getting our nails done?"

"Pedicures, actually," Nikki said, opening the glass door. Nikki was the last person I expected to get pedicures. Her feet were always covered in cowboy boots and usually mud. This had to be one of the weirdest things I'd heard.

The toxic smell of acrylics hit my nose as soon as we walked in, followed by the bright lights. I was used to going to salons back home with dim mood lighting and black, plush leather chairs. I wasn't expecting a very busty red headed woman to be behind a pink counter and to stop smacking her gum only long enough to greet us.

"Hey, y'all, welcome to House of Nails."

"Hey, Patsy," Nikki said, pushing her way between Blaine and me, which I was pretty sure she did on purpose. I had a feeling she still wanted him, even though he was obviously taken.

"Nikki Sinclair! I haven't seen you in ages! How you been?" Patsy stood up and wrapped Nikki in a big hug.

"I'm good. Just got done with finals, so figured I needed to come in for my monthly pedicure." Nikki held up her boot-clad foot.

"Cathy is just finishing up with someone, but I'll put you down to get her next."

Nikki nodded in my direction. "And my friends Blaine and Libby are going to be wanting one too."

Patsy's eyes roamed over Blaine a little too long for my liking. "This man wants a pedicure?"

Blaine shrugged. "Why not? Nikki swears by them, and my girl, here, is pregnant and I assume it won't be long before she can't see her toes and someone else will have to do them."

I swatted his arm. "Shut up! You didn't need to say that last part."

"Ouch! What? It's true."

Patsy put her arms out. "Don't worry nothing about that, honey. We'll just make sure to upgrade your pedicure so he'll be paying a little extra for you to get pampered. Every mama deserves one."

"Thank you," I said.

She smiled and sat back down behind the counter. "Okay, I'm going to put your names in, now you two ladies can go pick out your polishes, and you, sir, can head back to the chair on the far back wall and I'll have them meet you there."

"I guess I can do that," Blaine said, raising his eyebrows at me.

"Go on, go get your feet ready to be pampered," I said.

He shook his head. "If you tell the guys about this..."

Nikki laughed and picked up a pink polish from the rack on the wall. "Oh, they already know. Butch wants pictures."

"I hate you two so much right now."

Nikki just laughed. "And you'll love me again after this."

I turned away from her toward a rack of nail polish. I didn't like her using the 'L' word with my future husband. Sure, Blaine told me they were beyond over and he was marrying me, but I still couldn't help the jealousy that creeped in. Especially since it had been months since we'd had sex and I was pretty sure it would be real easy for him to hop back on the Nikki train if he wanted to.

And I really hoped he didn't.

"Oh, that's a pretty color," Nikki said, reaching over and lifting the purple nail polish that was in front of me.

I smiled. "No offense, but I don't see you as much of a purple girl. Of course I didn't see you as the type of girl to get pedicures either."

Nikki smirked. "Yeah, we all have our surprises."

I grabbed a pink polish off the wall and followed her toward the back. I was just thankful she took the chair on one side of Blaine and didn't try and sit in the middle. Though she did make sure I was the one sitting against the wall.

"Okay, now I see why you ladies do this." Blaine leaned back in his chair, pressing the different buttons that made it massage his back. A lady was at his feet, putting salts in the hot water where his feet were soaking.

"I told you these were relaxing," Nikki said, leaning back on her chair as a woman turned on the water.

I was the last one to have anyone come over to me. It was a younger girl who barely even looked at me. "Did you pick out your color?" she asked, turning on the water, not bothering to ask me if it was too hot. Which it was stifling, but I usually liked it when it burned a little.

"Yeah, it's right here." I held up the little pink bottle.

She nodded and took it from me, setting it on a small, wheeled cart where the rest of her tools were.

"Did you want to get your done in pink to match, Blaine?" Nikki asked.

"Naw, I'm good. I mean I don't need to have them painted a color, do I?"

I smiled. "Only if you want to."

Blaine laughed. "I had a feeling that if we had a girl I'd be in for a lot of toenail painting and hair doing. Now at least I get mudding and fishing."

I raised an eyebrow. "What if he takes after his mom and enjoys shopping and pedicures?"

Nikki cackled. "I don't think that's going to be the kind of boy that Blaine raises."

I leaned forward and glared at Nikki. "Hello? It's going to be both of us raising him. If my son wants to go shopping or wear a tutu then he can. He can do whatever he wants to."

"So you want to raise a homo?" Nikki asked.

"Wow, you really are a redneck hillbilly, you know that?" I snapped.

Blaine put his arms out. "Whoa, whoa. There is no need for any of this, girls. Can't we just relax and not fight for at least two seconds? I thought you two were cool."

Nikki leaned back and muttered something.

"What was that, Nik?" Blaine asked.

"Nothing, just thinking that the water feels nice," she said.

I leaned back in my own chair and pulled out one of the outdated People magazines on the table next to me. If this was supposed to be a relaxing trip, then I was going to do my best to avoid Nikki for as long as possible.

When we were done with our pedicures, we all walked out to our cars and I mumbled a goodbye to Nikki before slumping into the passenger seat. Blaine got in and started the car. "Well, that wasn't what I expected."

"What did you expect? That we were all going to hold hands and sing and everything would be A-okay?"

He shook his head. "Why can't you try and get along with her? I thought everything was good between y'all."

I blew out a breath. "Blaine, nothing is ever going to be okay with me and one of your exes. We tolerate each other but we're never going to be besties."

He sighed. "You're probably right. I shouldn't have put you two together. She just suggested the pedicure thing and I felt like I had to invite her. I didn't know it would cause a big hurricane."

"Well, now you know."

He glanced at me out of the corner of his eye. "You know she was trying. It wouldn't hurt you to try a little harder too."

I laughed and shook my head. "Blaine, I'm so big that I'm popping out of all of my pants, I have a baby that's practicing to be on the Olympic swim team in my stomach, and I've got my mother coming in tomorrow. I'm under a lot of stress and I don't' want another thing to have to worry about."

He frowned. "You know you're not the only one under a lot of stress, baby, we're in this together. It's not just you."

"But it is me. I'm the one who is sacrificing my body to bring a baby into the world. I'm the one who has to put my dreams on hold so that we can get married and I can take care of the baby until I go back to school."

The tires screeched as Blaine pulled the car over to the side of the road and slammed it into park. He stared at me, his eyes blazing. "What the hell, Lib? You think you're all alone in this? Don't you think I'm helping? Don't you realize all of the things I'm sacrificing? I've gone to every doctor's appointment, put a deposit down on a house, hell I wouldn't have asked you to marry me if I wasn't helping."

I crossed my arms over my chest. "So marrying me is just helping me out? You don't really want to?"

He shook his head. "Now, baby, I didn't mean it that way."

"But that's what you said, so some of it must have some meaning."

He groaned. "Baby, look, I know that you're frustrated and hormonal and whatever else, but you've gotta know that I'm here for you. No, I can't carry our son for you, but I can do everything I can to help you out and I have been. If there is something more that I can do, just say the word and I'll do it."

I didn't know I was crying until the tears fell down my cheeks in big heavy puddles, then I was uncontrollably sobbing. Blaine unbuckled his seatbelt and reached over the seat, pulling me to his chest as I soaked through his shirt with my tears.

He didn't say anything. He just rubbed my back and let me cry until I cried it all out and finally sniffled, looking up at him. "Thank you, Blaine. Sorry about that."

He kissed my forehead. "Sometimes we all need a good cry."

I shook my head. "Maybe I should just cry instead of being a bitch."

He wiped my cheeks. "No, I don't want to see your tears because of me ever again, even though I know it's going to happen, I'll try everything I can to make sure that it doesn't."

Another surge of tears fell down my cheeks.

"Aw, baby, why are you crying now?" He pulled me close to him.

"Because you say the nicest things to me and I'm just a hormonal bitch."

He laughed, his chest rumbling against my cheek. "Naw, I wouldn't go that far baby. You're growing another human and sometimes that just messes with your emotion. I'll cut you some slack."

"Not too much, though, I don't want to be one of those bitter moms," I said.

He kissed my forehead. "I promise."

Chapter 16

My mom's flight got in early the next morning. I wished I didn't have to get up that early to pick her up, but I didn't want to just tell her to take a cab either. I was hoping I'd be able to squeeze a nap in later on in the day.

When I pulled up to the arrival gates, I had to honk the horn a few times before she finally nodded and ran over to my car.

"Sorry, I didn't recognize your new car!" she said, putting her arms out for a hug.

"Yeah, figured that wasn't the best for a family car."

She wheeled her suitcase into the back seat. "And you've gotten so big! I think your stomach is at least twice the size as it was at Christmas! Your little boy is growing!"

I winced, but kept my back to her as I got in the car. I hated when people told pregnant women that. I knew it was supposed to be a compliment, but it never felt right to for people to tell me how huge I was.

"This isn't bad for a moderately priced sedan," Mom said, running her hand along the armrest.

It was probably supposed to be a compliment and I was starting to wonder if I sounded like her when I talked.

"I like it. It gets me around." I pulled out of the space and went toward the highway. "So, do you want me to drop you off at your hotel?"

"Why don't we run by there so I can check in, then we can grab a quick bite before heading out to some of those boutiques on Magazine Street and see if they have something in your style for dresses?"

I forced the biggest smile I could. I knew she was there to spend time with me and finish wedding preparations. I also knew that she really wanted to go dress shopping, but I still hated the thought of it. "Sure, Mom, that sounds great."

I DIDN'T EXPECT WEDDING dress shopping that afternoon, nor did I expect my mom to have set up an appointment at one of the upscale wedding boutiques on Magazine Street.

I should have known better.

The shop looked innocent enough from the outside with its small wooden sign and dress display in the large window in the front.

Then I walked inside, and weddingness threw up.

It was not only a wedding dress shop, but one that sold invitations, programs, and just about everything else one would need in paper for a wedding. I was just glad that Aunt Dee and her team of scrapbookers made invitations that were simple yet chic and we were able to mail all of those out at the beginning of May. If not, I was sure my mom would find the most expensive ones she could in some silken paper and insist we get them.

A woman in a tailored black suit with her blonde hair pulled back into a high ponytail approached us. "Hello, my name is Chelsea, how may I help you today?"

Mom smiled, putting her arm around me. "Hi, Chelsea, I'm Kathryn and this is my daughter, Libby. We have an appointment for today at two."

The woman's face contorted into something that sort of resembled a smile. "Yes, I remember talking to you on the phone, it's a pleasure meeting you and Libby."

She shook both our hands and I caught her eyes grazing down toward my stomach. I only had a salad for lunch and was wearing a dark blue peasant top and maxi skirt that I thought were flowy enough to not to draw too much attention to my middle. I guess I was wrong when my mother and the sales lady couldn't take their eyes off of my stomach.

"Okay, is there any particular style you're looking for? Color?" Chelsea asked, moving her hands with each word.

"Um, white?" I said, even though I maybe should have looked at something in red since the way she was looking at me, I wasn't feeling so pure.

She did that thing with her lips again that looked like she was trying her hardest to force a small. "White or off white or maybe cream or pearl?"

I shrugged. "It doesn't matter too much."

"She's getting married June 11th in a Catholic church with an outdoor reception on his family's farm, so something that would go along with that theme," Mom said, squeezing my shoulder.

Blaine's family didn't have a farm. Not even close. It was more like a bunch of land and some swamp. But I didn't correct her.

Chelsea nodded. "Okay. I think we can find some sample dresses here that could work and then you could take one home today if you like it."

"That sounds wonderful!" Mom gushed.

Chelsea led us over to a rack and strummed through a few dresses. "Now, do you know your size or would you like me to measure you?"

"Um, last time I wore a dress it was a six, but that was in August," I muttered the last part.

"I see," Chelsea said and grabbed a long pink strand that looked like ribbon from a table. "Do you mind if I take a few measurements just so we get it correct?"

"Uh, yeah, go ahead?"

She put the measuring tape around my chest, arms, and legs and took way too long measuring my middle. "Okay, it looks like we may want to go with a ten. Possibly a twelve. Yeah I think a twelve would be good unless you want more room to expand."

"A WHAT?" My eyes bugged out of my head.

"Libby, it's okay. You're carrying a baby. I wish I was still that small when I was pregnant with you," Mom said, rubbing my back.

"Yeah, and I still have four months to go. Who knows how big I'll be by then."

Chelsea's lips twinged. "I do have a few tens and twelves in some samples. Why don't I pick them out for you and you head back with your mother to the dressing room. It's where that purple curtain is." She pointed toward a corner wall.

"Thanks, we'll do that," Mom said, putting her arm around me and guiding me toward the dressing room.

"This is going to be fun," I muttered.

Mom sighed. "Can you just humor me a little? I know you really don't want to do this, but you do need a dress. You can't exactly go naked down the aisle...even though that's exactly how this all started, isn't it?"

"Mom!"

She laughed. "Oh, you know I'm just playing around, but seriously, for me? I came all this way to help my daughter pick out a wedding dress, so let's do it."

I sighed as Chelsea came forward and hung a few dresses on the wall next to the curtained off corner that I guess was supposed to be the dressing room. "Okay, Libby, I have a few different styles for you to try on. Just let me know if you need a different size or some shoes, or anything else."

"Will do," I said and closed the curtain, peering at the dresses in front of me.

One looked like a giant white bed sheet that had a big bow tied over the boobs. Another looked like a white shag rug, and the last two looked like other renditions of sheets with flowers or jewels on them.

None of them looked like the dresses I pictured when I thought I'd someday be walking down the aisle. Not that I was always the girl that dreamed about her wedding, but now that it was actually about to happen, I just couldn't see myself in a sheet.

The first two sheets I tried on didn't fit so I resorted to the last sheet and the shag carpet. Both just made me look like an awkward pregnant woman.

Mom thanked Chelsea for her time, but didn't say anything about us coming back. I expected her to suggest another store, but instead she just walked to the car and sat in the passenger seat. I got in next to her and buckled my seat belt.

"The last time I saw you this worked up over dresses was when we were buying your dress for the Alpha Mu formal," Mom said, looking down at her fingernails.

"Yeah, that was a mess."

I went with my ex-boyfriend to his fraternity formal. My mom and I spent all spring break going to every store in Chicago to find a dress and ended up just getting a little black dress at The Limited. That night my date puked on it and then I caught him hooking up with another chick.

"That was when I first noticed you had a problem. I mean, I guess I always knew that you were pushing your food around on your plate or would spend an extra long time in the bathroom, but the way you would stare at your body in the mirror and curl your lip in disgust no matter how gorgeous you looked in the dress, that was when I took notice."

"Mom, that was months ago. I'm better now. I've been getting counseling and the nutritionist even has me on a plan for pregnant women."

She shook her head. "You know, your body is different now. You're growing a person inside of you. All the curves and changes are because you are creating life."

I stared down at my stomach. "It's just hard to see it sometimes."

Mom put her hand on mine. "I know. This must be so difficult for you to not equate what you see in the mirror with what it is. But, Libby, you are beautiful, even while pregnant. Your body is changing, and you know what? It's not going to go back to normal. You may have stretch marks, you may have scars, but they're all a badge of honor into motherhood. You probably don't understand it all now, but you will. And if you need anyone to talk to, I'm always here. Beth too."

I bit my bottom lip to try and keep my emotions at bay. I didn't know if I believed all of it right now, but just having someone tell me it was okay was all I needed. I never had that when I was struggling with my body issues in college. It was always about how I fit into something, now I had to come to grips with the fact that it wasn't just me that needed my body. It was one hell of a concept.

"Thanks, Mom."

AFTER DROPPING MOM back off at her hotel, I headed to Aunt Dee's. Mom offered for me to stay with her, but I just wanted to curl up in my own bed for a while.

When I got in Aunt Dee was in the kitchen. "Hey, honey, did you find a dress?"

My face fell as soon as I made the few steps from the living room to the counter. "No. We didn't. Kind of hard to find something for a pregnant woman or just me in general."

Aunt Dee frowned. "You know, I could always make you something if you found a pattern. I do still have the sewing machine up in the closet in my bedroom."

I shook my head. "I couldn't ask you to do that."

"Or..." She walked out of the room before even finishing her thought, only to emerge about a minute later with a giant white box.

"What's that?" I asked, following her to the kitchen table where she set it down.

"This is my dress."

She opened the box and slowly pulled out a long sleeved lace dress with a satin bow tied around the middle. "Now it may not be your style, but if we capped the sleeves, shortened it and I loosened it to make it a wrap style, I think it would look beautiful."

I shook my head. "Aunt Dee, I couldn't ask you to do that to your dress."

Even as I said the words, I knew I didn't mean them. It was the first time I could actually imagine myself wearing anything, just from the way she described how she could transform it.

She smiled. "Joni never got to wear my dress and if Britt still wants to wear it, I can keep all the scraps and alter it again. I want you to wear it. It would mean so much to me."

I couldn't stop the happy tears that streamed from my eyes. "Okay, Aunt Dee. I will."

Chapter 17

Another reason why Mom came to Louisiana was to finally meet Blaine's family and help finalize wedding plans. This, of course, meant a big dinner at The Crabtrees'.

And, in true Crabtree fashion, when I pulled up to the house with my mom in the passenger seat, Abby was standing completely naked on the front porch and yelling at the top of her lungs while her siblings splashed around in a blow up pool beside her, all completely naked.

I glanced at my mom, wincing in anticipation of her reaction to my new country bumpkin family. But instead of looking horrified, she laughed. "Well, I guess that's one way to cool down in the south."

"Usually Abby is in a tutu." I pulled the car to the side and put it in park, cutting the engine.

"I'm sure being naked and yelling is much more comfortable."

I sighed. "Mom, I should warn you, The Crabtrees'...well...they aren't exactly..." I racked my brain, searching for the right word. I was never the best with words and pregnancy brain had hit me in full force. Half the times I couldn't even remember what I was going to say, so I just smiled.

Mom put her hand on mine. "I'm sure they're fine. You act like I'm some snob that's going to turn my nose up at everything. Lighten up, Lib. I was young once too."

I smiled, but really couldn't imagine my mom being the type of lady who would go mudding with the Crabtrees, but then again I couldn't see myself doing that either.

"Libby! Mrs. Gentry! You made it!" Blaine hopped over the side railing and came barreling toward the car. He may have been wearing his Sunday best button down and khakis, but there was no way anyone could take the wild boy out of him.

"I wanna jump over the rail like Uncle Blaine too!" Abby whined and hoisted her leg up, but dropped it again as soon as it was in the air.

"Abigail Mae, you put your leg down and put your swimsuit back on!" Meg's scratchy voice yelled as she came onto the porch.

Meg waved in our direction. "Sorry about my heathen children."

Mom smiled and approached the small pool where the kids were running in circles. "It's no trouble at all. I remember when Libby and her sister were that young. I couldn't keep them in clothes and it became a real problem when they started nursery school."

Meg laughed, breaking the tension. At least Mom broke the ice with one family member, but there were still a lot more to go.

Alicia came outside with her daughter, Callie, balanced on her hip. The five-month-old was starting to look more like her dad with her dark curls and huge blue eyes. "Hey, you must be Libby's mama." She embraced my mom in a huge hug.

At first my mom didn't hug back and the shocked look on her face said she wasn't expecting it, but then she slowly melted into her and hugged her too. Mom then pulled back and tickled Callie's toes, which caused her to laugh. "There are so many babies around here! It's wonderful! I just had my first grand-daughter in March."

Alicia smiled. "Yeah and she's going to be the little flower girl, I'm told."

"Hey! I thought I was going to be the flower girl!" Abby whined.

"You are, Abby, now shush!" Meg swatted her butt after pulling up her pink swim bottoms.

I smiled down at Abby. "Remember you and Braiden have the big job of pulling Luxx in the wagon."

"Ohhh...yeah!" Abby nodded and poked my belly. "And what about your baby?"

"He won't be here in time for the wedding, but you'll get to meet him soon."

"Mama said we were having this wedding because of your baby, so if we're going to all this fuss then why isn't he here?" Abby asked, putting her hands on her hips.

A blush crept up Meg's face as she scooped Abby up. "Abby, what did Mama tell you about talking like that?"

"What? It's what you and Daddy said! You said because Libby's having a baby, they're having a shotgun wedding. Are there going to be guns and fireworks?"

Meg's face grew redder. "I'm going to take Abby inside and get her changed before supper, excuse me."

"Well, that wasn't awkward at all," Blaine whispered and put his arm around me.

"Why don't we head inside? I'm sure Ma and Dad are ready to meet you, Mrs. Gentry," Alicia said.

Blaine's dad and brother-in-laws were crowded in the tiny living room around the TV as usual when we walked in. Blaine's Dad gave his usual pleasantries and then went back to watching TV. Then we walked into the dining room where Meemaw was camped out in her favorite chair at the head of the table, her oxygen tank sitting beside her and the usual scowl on her face.

"Hey, Meemaw, this is Libby's mama, Kathryn. She's here for supper tonight," Blaine said, waving his hands at Mom like he was Vanna White.

Meemaw's face softened a bit as Mom gave her hand. "It's nice to meet you, Mrs. Crabtree."

Meemaw patted Mom's hand. "Libby is a very lovely girl. My Blaine is lucky to have her."

My jaw practically dropped to the floor. I didn't think that Meemaw liked me, let alone thought I was good for Blaine. The woman didn't say much to me unless she was wanting me to get out of her way so she could go smoke.

Mom smiled. "We're very lucky to have Blaine and she's very grateful for you and your family."

Meemaw stared off wistfully. "They remind me of myself and my late husband, Abel. I was pregnant with Arthur's older brother at that time, but we lost him shortly after the wedding."

I blinked once then twice. I didn't know any of that about Meemaw and just hearing about it brought tears to my eyes and I found myself reaching for my stomach, just to make sure it was still there. Blaine must have felt the same way because his hand was on mine the instant I moved it.

"I'm very sorry about your loss, Mrs. Crabtree. Even today that must be still hard," Mom said. She was the best at empathizing. It's why she killed it in the courtroom with witnesses.

Meemaw smiled and looked at my mom. "That was decades ago. Now we're onto new life and new happiness."

"That we are Meemaw, That we are," Blaine said and kissed my forehead.

DINNER AT THE CRABTREES' was always an adventure.

Before Vicki, Meg, and Alicia could even finish setting the table, Abby already threw a fairy wand into the potato salad and Braiden knocked down the plate of cornbread while the dogs happily gobbled it up.

I thought Mom would be mortified but she laughed and even helped pick up the empty plates.

After prayers were said, and everyone gobbled down dinner, the boys retreated to the living room, and Mom and I helped clean up dinner.

Since we mostly got takeout at my parents' or threw everything in the dishwasher, I'd never actually seen my mom clear a table, let alone rinse and dry dishes after Vicki washed them.

After everything was cleared, Mom and I sat down at the table with Vicki. Meemaw was still there, sitting in the corner and staring out the window. I thought about asking her if she needed anything, but no one else did and I didn't know if this was just what she did.

"Okay, so let's talk wedding," Mom said, taking the seat next to me.

"Well, what do you want to know?" Vicki asked, folding her hands together on the table.

"Everything," Mom said. "Tell me the menu. What you still need. Anything at all that you need."

Vicki smiled. "I don't know if Libby told you, but it's kind of a tradition that all of us women get together to make the meal. Dee's offered to help as well so we'll be working on that Friday night, getting it set up and then after the wedding, the ladies from the church will come in and help us heat up the food and serve the meal."

"And what are we having?"

Vicki's face fell. "It's nothing fancy. I'm sure it's nothing like your Chicago dinners, but Libby and Blaine wanted to do a crawfish boil with cornbread and red beans and rice. And of course wedding cake and a king cake for Blaine's groom's cake."

"That all sounds wonderful, Vicki. You have done so much work. Are you sure there isn't anything more I can do? Rent the tables and linens? Anything?"

Vicki smiled. "Trust me, Kathryn, you've done enough for us. Your generosity has helped us out more than you know."

I raised an eyebrow at the smile they shared between them. I knew Mom said that they were talking, but I wondered exactly what Mom was helping them out with.

"Have you bought your dress yet?" Mom asked.

Vicki shook her head. "No, I think I'll probably just wear something that I have."

Mom waved her hand. "Nonsense, your only son is getting married. We should go into New Orleans tomorrow and pick you out something new."

"Oh, that won't be necessary. I'm sure I can find something. Maybe I'll head into one of the boutiques in Caimon."

"Oh, Lenora's? That's where we are going tomorrow to pick out the bridesmaid dresses. You should join us!" Mom clasped her hands together.

Vicki waved her hands. "Oh, no. That isn't necessary."

"Please, I insist."

Vicki chewed on her bottom lip and wrung her hands together, looking at me like I'd give the answer. This wasn't the usual, brassy Vicki I was used to.

"Oh, stop pussyfooting around and just say you'll go with the woman!" Meemaw yelled.

Vicki blinked quickly and I had to hold back a laugh.

"Okay. I guess I'm going with y'all to Lenora's."

WHILE ELSBURY HAD A downtown that consisted of one block of businesses, Caimon was a quaint, country setting.

There were little shops that sold things like candles and homemade jam that blended right alongside the brick facade of the post office and library. It was something that Elsbury could have used more of, but trying to convince the good ol' boys that ran the town of that was easier said than done.

"This is very chic!" Mom said as soon as we got out of the car and stepped onto the sidewalk. Britt followed behind us. Britt hadn't said a word the whole way. Granted, she didn't talk too much as it was, but when my mom was around she was virtually silent.

"Yeah. It's cute."

"Did you and Blaine look for a place around here? This looks very you."

It didn't look "me". It didn't feel "me". Caimon was pretty and filled with things that were Southern and people tried to put their own spin on it to make it cutesy, like Mason jars with burlap ribbons and pastel bow ties. I felt like I was more of the opposite, like the new car that was now tarnished with rust.

I'd come a long way in learning to accept myself and realize that I could be loved, but there were a lot of days that I found myself questioning everything. I never thought at twenty years old that I'd be pregnant, living in the south, and getting married in a maternity wedding dress.

I was in a better place than I was back home in Chicago, though. When I was in college, I was living a lie of being the girl who tried to fit in. The girl who threw up every meal to wear a new pair of jeans. In Louisiana, I could actually eat seconds and wear last season's shoes and not feel like I was going to be judged.

But sometimes old habits die hard.

"Yeah. It is cute, but a little far from work for Blaine and from school for me."

Mom squeezed my hand and then opened the glass door to the shop. The cool air was a welcome relief from the May heat that was already sweltering.

While the bridal shop on Magazine Street was put-together and matchy-matchy, Lenora's was a little bit more of a kitschy free-for-all with dark hard wood floors, lime green walls, and zebra furniture that was randomly placed around the room between racks of dresses.

"Libby! You're here!" Dina ran over to me, her heels clicking on the floor. I didn't know why she needed the high-heeled strappy sandals, or the flowered sundress. With her makeup painted on and her hair in a French twist, she looked like she was going out for a date instead of dress shopping. "And you must be Libby's mom. Howdy. I'm Dina."

"Pleasure to meet you, Dina. I've heard so much about you," Mom said, shaking her hand back politely.

The bell rang over the door and we turned around to see Alicia and Meg walk in with Abby on Meg's arm. Slowly coming in behind them was Vicki's mom.

"You're here!" Mom said, wrapping her arms around Vicki like they were old friends.

Vicki hugged her bag, but her face looked like she was about to burst at any moment. My mom could be a little overbearing.

I pulled her back. "Down, Mom. I know you found a new friend, but you could reel it in a bit."

Mom frowned at me.

"Sorry," I mouthed, half to her and half to Vicki.

A woman came out from behind a purple curtain at the back of the store. While the boutique on Magazine Street had a polished professional, this woman was a little bit more my speed with her jeans and plain white t-shirt, her dark hair in a loose bun. "Oh, it looks like y'all are here! I'm guessing this is the Gentry-Crabtree bridal party?"

I nodded and stepped forward shaking her hand. "Yes, I'm Libby."

She smiled, lighting up her whole face. "Pleasure to meet you, Libby. I'm Meledy."

Her eyes didn't roam over my stomach like everyone else's usually did, instead it stayed on my face and I knew that I instantly liked her.

"So, how many bridesmaids do we have? And what are you looking for?" She clasped her hands together.

"I have six, but two are back in Chicago. And two flower girls. I'm thinking shades of purple. Like a dark purple. Eggplant? If it's not all the same style that's okay with me too."

She tapped her fingers on her chin and hummed as if she was making mental notes. "Okay. That would be a lot of fun if we did the same shade and had each girl pick out their own dress. I can even get the brand and exact color if you want to send it to your bridesmaids in Chicago."

I grinned. "That would be perfect."

She looked at the girls behind me. "Why don't y'all start looking through the racks here and see what we have in dark purple that you like and we can start trying them on. Do a little fashion show?"

The girls looked between each other and then shrugged before they scattered, going to the different racks.

"I hope you don't mind. I don't want to seem pushy," Meledy said.

I shook my head. "No. It's perfect. Low key. It's how I like it."

"You're not making us wear heels, are you?" Alicia yelled.

"I guess you don't have to. You could wear flats," I said.

Meledy grasped my arm. "You know what would be really cute? Feel free to say 'no', but if all the girls were in purple dresses with brown cowboy boots. It would definitely have that country feel."

I hadn't thought about that. I never actually thought about having cowboy boots at a wedding, but I assumed Blaine would be in his boots. The guys were wearing jeans with brown blazers and white button-ups, so girls in boots would actually match well.

"Yeah. That would be great." I couldn't help the grin that kept spreading on my face. It was the most I smiled in a while. Finally things were looking up with this wedding planning.

"You know, there are a lot of cute things in this store, maybe you could actually find some maternity clothes that fit you," Mom said, leaning over my shoulder.

"Oh, I don't need any." I shook my head.

Meledy smiled. "You know, I did just get in some new tops if you just wanted to try them out. They're not exactly maternity, but with the flowy material, you can wear them now and even after the baby is born."

I looked between my mom and Meledy's smiling faces and then sighed. "Okay. You two win."

It was way easier shopping with all of the girls than I thought it would be. Even Brittany found a purple high-lo dress that looked great with boots. It was only the second time I'd seen her in a dress and the first time I'd seen her happy to be in one.

Vicki finally eased up and picked out a light brown shift dress and I walked away with a few tops and dresses, and of course new boots.

I wasn't sure if I could get the nerve to wear something in a bigger size, but after trying them on and actually feeling comfortable instead of like I was about to burst out of my clothes, I decided it was time. It also helped that Meledy wasn't pushy and everything seemed to finally be falling into place in my life.

Now I just hoped it stayed that way.

Chapter 18

After dress shopping, I left with my mom the next morning to fly back to Chicago.

Aunt Dee wasn't done with my dress and on the plane ride, in my new maxi dress from Lenora's, I was wondering if maybe I should have picked out another dress while we were getting the ones for the bridesmaids, or maybe considered looking somewhere in Chicago.

But another part of me, knew she could pull it off. If I could pull of school, a baby, and a marriage, I had to have faith that everything was going to fall into place.

I would have preferred a day to relax and just put my feet up, but my time in Chicago was short and I was cramming in two baby slash bridal showers, a bachelorette party, bridesmaid and flower girl dress shopping with Beth, and anything else my mother could find to do.

After an early morning flight, I barely had time to change before we drove to Beth's place in the suburbs.

I hadn't seen her and barely talked to her since Luxx was born. The last time I talked to her, she was half paying attention to me and constantly complaining about Luxx's latch on her boob. Obviously our conversation didn't last long.

Beth and Brian lived in one of the large suburbs that was about a forty-five minute drive from the city and a ten minute drive from the house we grew up in. Brian was a chiropractor at a clinic in town and Beth taught at the local elementary school, but was taking the rest of the year and the summer off to spend time with Luxx. I secretly wondered if she was actually ever going to go back to work. She was always the more maternal one out of the two of us. When we played house when we were younger, she was always the mommy, toting all of her dolls wherever we went. I was the one who preferred to see how many of the dolls I could stuff in random places and then wait to hear Beth scream when she found them.

Now we were both having little babies of our own. This time I wouldn't be the one hiding my kid in random places. Now I actually had to be "the mommy".

Cars were already parked in the driveway and up and down the oak-lined street. Their house looked like something that a movie would be filmed at with the Frank Lloyd Wright design (that I only knew what it was called because Beth never shut up about it when they first bought it). I thought it was kind of weird looking with the heavy window sills, pointed wide roof overhang, and the dark gray stucco that completed the house.

But who was I to judge? I was going to be living in a shotgun house in New Orleans.

Not that I was complaining. I loved that Blaine loved the house and that it was going to be close to work and school, but it wasn't what I dreamed of in a home. I never really thought too much about my future and forever afters but now that it was happening, I thought about sitting on the front porch in the summer time, drinking sweet tea, and watching kids play in the yard. There wasn't a yard in the New Orleans house or even a real porch.

Maybe someday.

Mom parked and we walked down the flower-lined path to Beth's front door, where a spring wreath hung that said "welcome" in big, curvy letters.

We didn't even need to ring the doorbell. Beth was already at it, staring at us wide-eyed.

"Thank God you're here!" She hugged me and Mom.

I raised an eyebrow. "Is everything okay?"

Beth pulled back and looked at me. "Have you talked to Leslie lately?"

I shook my head.

Beth nodded toward the living room to her left. "You may want to go see her. Or not. You could go run back outside too."

Okay, this was getting weirder and now I had to see.

I slipped my shoes off and walked into Beth's professionally decorated living room with the beige walls and white furniture. I expected maybe some puke on the ground from a baby or something that showed she had children.

But instead of paying attention to the cute little bow tie garland or Mason jars full of baby toys, I saw Leslie, sitting in the middle of a few people on the couch with her hands on a growing baby bump.

Mom stopped beside me and froze. It wasn't until Leslie finally looked in our direction that we were forced to move. And move very slowly.

"Libby! The guest of honor!" Leslie stood up and walked over to us, giving us both a hug.

"Leslie, you're...you..." I just stared. I couldn't even form words.

Leslie waved her hands. "Oh, let's not talk about me right now. This is your day. It's your wedding and baby shower!"

"And I guess we'll have to start planning one for you as well?" I asked, still staring.

Leslie's hands flitted to her stomach. "Oh, we don't need to talk about that."

"I think we kind of do. When did this happen?" Mom asked.

Leslie forced a smile. "We found out when Libby was here last, but we weren't sure we wanted to tell anyone just yet, especially with all the excitement of Luxx and Libby being here. We also thought about adoption, but once we saw that little heartbeat, there was no way that Clifton and I could ever part with her. We're due in October."

One month after me. Holy shit, my baby was going to have an aunt or uncle that was his age. This was not what I was expecting to hear when I came to Beth's. I didn't know whether to be pissed off or sad or what. Instead, I was just in shock.

"Oh. Wow. That's crazy and I'm so happy for the two of you!" I said, mustering up the biggest smile I could force.

"I need to go feed Luxx before the shower starts," Beth said, scooting toward the baby swing that was swaying back and forth.

"Oh, do you mind if I watch? I've been doing research on breast feeding and it would help me to see a proper latch. Maybe Libby wants to see as well," Leslie asked, blinking slowly.

"Um, well, I'm still not very good at it. We've been doing a lot of supplementing." Beth's eyes darted around the room as if she was looking for her escape.

"Oh. That's okay. I understand," Leslie said, rubbing her stomach and then walking back to the party where a few of my cousins and aunts were sitting.

None of my friends were there yet, but they were supposed to come after the shower for the bachelorette party. I wasn't even sure if I actually wanted a bachelorette party. I was still under twenty-one, so I couldn't technically get into the bars, ignoring my fake ID, and pretty sure it would be frowned upon to be the pregnant woman rolling up to the bar, even if I just drank virgin pina coladas all night.

My mom's cousin, Ellen, scooted over for a spot for me on the couch. "Elizabeth Gentry, I haven't seen you in ages."

"It's been awhile." I smiled. I actually didn't see too much of my family. Mom was an only child and my dad had an older brother who lived in Canada. We had some scattered cousins around, but nothing like the Crabtree family gatherings.

"I know. I think my high school graduation was the last time."

She pursed her lips. "Yes. That would make sense. But now look at you! Getting married, having a baby, living in New Orleans. It's like you're a whole different person."

"Yeah. I guess you could say that." I didn't know if it was supposed to be an insult or not. Ellen had a face that I liked to call "resting bitch face"; she rarely smiled and it just looked like she was always pissed off at the world.

"Do you have a name picked out?" my mom's cousin, Brenda, poked her head out from behind Ellen.

"Not exactly, but we have some ideas."

"Well, go on, spill them!" Brenda said.

"Blaine really likes the name William Robert Crabtree, but I'm still not sure. I'm thinking of something more original, yet traditional."

Beth came practically out of nowhere with a sleeping Luxx in her arms. "You know that William Robert would be shortened to Billy Bob, right?"

"What?" I raised an eyebrow.

"Bill is short for William and Bob is short for Robert, ergo Billy Bob. You'd definitely have a country boy if you named him that."

Everyone in the room laughed as if I was the butt of some kind of a cruel joke and I wasn't exactly pleased by it. As if Mom could sense my dismay, she clasped her hands and approached the group. "Ladies, why don't we get this party started now that we're all here?"

But I didn't want to party. I didn't want to do anything. People always talked about post-partum depression, but I felt like I was getting pre-baby depression. My hormones were all over the place, so I would get upset if I dropped a plate or stubbed my toe. I could cry at the freaking drop of a hat. Now, I had to smile and pretend like I wanted to be with everyone, when really I was ready to sleep.

After a light lunch of finger sandwiches and salads that were all catered in from some upscale cafe, we drank blue lemonade from plastic cups decorated with mustaches.

Then I had to sit my big pregnant butt in a chair and open various baby and wedding gifts while Beth wrote them all down. Then people marked them off a check list for a baby and wedding dual bingo game that Beth found on Pinterest.

Sure, I spent the whole day sitting, but by the time my last family member left, I was exhausted. I wanted nothing more than to go back to my parents' house, curl up in their expensive guest bed and sleep the rest of the week.

But Beth had other plans.

After another feeding with Luxx, she passed her and a diaper bag off to my mom.

"Luxx isn't going to stay for her first bachelorette party?" I asked as Beth shut the door behind Mom.

Beth shook her head. "Very funny. The only baby allowed is my nephew Billy Bob and he has to stay in your stomach because there is no way in hell I want to deal with labor tonight."

"Aw, darn, so Leslie isn't coming back?"

Beth stopped and put her hands on her hips. "Can we just talk about how messed up it is that our step-grandma is having a baby who will be younger than both of ours?"

I shook my head. "How about the fact that none of us knew until today? I wonder what Dad is going to say when Mom tells him."

Beth shrugged. "Nothing that I'd want to say out loud and probably a lot of uses of the F word."

"As long as he doesn't go back to downing a bottle of alcohol because of it," I muttered.

"What was that?"

"Nothing. Just talking to myself."

Beth shook her head and sat down next to me. "You know, my friends used to all think we had the greatest life. We had the big house, nice cars, and our parents were still together. They didn't know that when our Dad got off work every night, he would pour himself a drink and then keep drinking until he passed out on the couch. It's why I never had anyone over and lost a lot of friends because of it."

I remembered all of that vividly. Dad wasn't a bad guy, he just drank...a lot. I just thought it was normal. That a lot of parents had that stress. When I went to college, I figured that was how people dealt with their daily stress was to drink to excess. Now, after spending months with a counselor and actually being happy in Louisiana, I realized that drinking to excess wasn't the best way to handle things. Of course, neither was me crying about everything.

"I was really worried when Brian and I found out we were pregnant. I didn't want Dad to watch Luxx and have him pass out while she drowned in the bath tub or electrocuted herself. I had a long talk with Mom and Dad and said that he had to get sober or they weren't going to see Luxx."

I raised my eyebrows. "Wow. That's pretty harsh, Beth."

She frowned. "But it needed to be said. I told them all that not long after you and Blaine went back to Louisiana. They were pissed at first, of course, and Dad said he didn't have a problem, but eventually he did straighten out. I think the same thing sort of happened when they found out about you and Blaine. I expected Dad to be pissed or get wasted, but instead he actually seemed happy. It was as if the joy of being a grandfather replaced his need to drink. I think Dad's actually happy now and maybe being happy helped him to overcome his demons."

"Wow, that's really philosophical of you, Beth."

It was. It took a lot of deep thinking and for the first time I found myself actually smiling. I expected Dad did go down a bottle after he found out I was pregnant, but maybe he didn't. Maybe all of the Gentry's were getting stronger.

She smacked my leg. "Shut up. I'm being serious."

I rubbed my leg. "Ow! I was being serious, too. It all makes sense to me, too. I guess you just voice things better than I can."

She smiled. "It's the teacher in me."

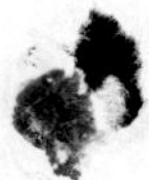

A FEW MINUTES LATER, Kristi rang the doorbell and came in with mixings for virgin cocktails and a few bottles of wine that she immediately put on ice.

"Libby! You look great!" She hugged me as soon as all of the drinks were put away.

"Thanks, Kristi, I feel like a whale. A very tired whale."

Kristi shook her head. "Girl, you've got to stop body shaming yourself! You've always been your worst critic and this is the time in your life when you can eat anything you want and it's okay to be big."

I chewed on my bottom lip. "Not exactly. The term eating for two isn't accurate because there isn't a full other person inside of me, but I am eating a few more calories than normal."

Kristi rolled her eyes. "Are you using an app to track it?"

"I am!" I said, pulling out my phone.

Kristi sight and shook her head. "You can't go through your whole life worried about your appearance or track it with an app. Do you ever just let your hair down and stop worrying about everything around you?"

I frowned. "Wow, Kristi, thanks for coming over and making me feel like shit."

She offered a sympathetic smile. "I just worry about you, lil sis. I know how you get about things and I just want to make sure you aren't going to have a nervous breakdown like I'm pretty sure you did during your first midterms."

I sighed, remembering the fact that I downed a bottle of tequila and ate an entire pizza, then threw it all up the night before my Spanish final. "No, Kristi. I'm not going to have a breakdown. Believe it or not, I'm happy. Things may be going crazy, but I have a good support system behind me."

She squeezed my shoulder. "Good. Keep that support system close and you know I'll always be a part of it. Even if I can be a bitch."

I smiled. "Thanks, Kris."

The doorbell rang and a few more of my sorority sisters came to the door, followed soon by some that had graduated, and the living room was full again. Beth brought out more finger foods while Kristi poured some wine.

"So what's the plan for tonight?" I asked, sipping on a Shirley Temple.

"You know, going downtown and all of us wear fake bellies to see how many dudes we can find that are into pregnant girls. Then we'll head down Belmont to the sex clubs and see how you look in leather," Beth said, keeping a straight face.

"Please tell me you're joking," I said.

"Maybe I am and maybe I'm not."

The doorbell rang again.

"Oh that must be the sex toy party host!" Kristi jumped up.

"Sex toy party?" I asked, raising an eyebrow at Beth.

She smiled. "Well, I had to think of something that wasn't bar hopping and there's nothing to say that you and Blaine still can't have some fun on your honeymoon."

"Gross, I don't want to talk about my sex life with my sister."

"Hey, we all know how you got pregnant, no shame in hiding it now."

"Uh, Beth, Libby, you'd better come to the door," Kristi yelled.

I raised an eyebrow and stood up, following Kristi to the door. My mouth dropped in shock when I saw two men in blue uniforms standing at the door. But the bigger shock was that one of them was my ex-boyfriend, Beau.

He whipped off his aviators and ran his hand through his spiky hair. "Excuse me, ma'am, we had a call about a noise complaint."

Beth's eyes widened. "Oh. Shit."

"Sorry, sir, we'll keep it down," I said.

The other cop entered, followed by Beau and slammed the door behind him. "Oh, I've got something you can keep down."

He ripped his shirt off, exposing a well-oiled set of washboard abs. Something told me this wasn't a real cop.

Hooting and hollering came from behind me as the song "Bad Boys" started blaring from behind the now shirtless cop. He put his hand on my chest and slowly pushed me backward until I found myself plopping on one of Beth's living room chairs.

Beau slid up next to him, ripping off his shirt and pants and throwing them behind me. At least the guy had been working out since college and his body was decent to look at, but I couldn't think about anything but the fact that I was face-to-head with his very tiny man thong as him and the other guy bumped and grinded on my lap.

I tried to squeeze my eyes shut, but it was like a damn train wreck and I couldn't look away. After what felt like the longest line of body rolls and pelvic thrusts, they were finally done. Their man thongs were full of dollar bills as they put their clothes back on.

I stood up from the chair and found Beau standing directly beside me with a big smile on his face. "Hey, didn't know this was going to be your bachelorette party. Looks like things have gone pretty well with you and the redneck...really well." His eyes roamed down to my stomach.

"Yes. They are. Is that why you're here? To rub this all in my face? Pun intended," I snapped. I was tired, my feet hurt, and I was pretty sure I had a bruise on my forehead from his police badge that was attached to the stupid man thong.

Beth put her hand on my shoulder. "Libby, I had no idea he was going to be the stripper that showed up."

Beau shook his head. "No, I didn't either. When the agency gave me the address and said it was for Beth Watterson, I completely forgot it was your sister's name."

I blew out a deep breath. Figured. Beau could barely remember his own sister's new last name, let alone mine.

"It still doesn't explain why a guy, who had a job downtown, is stripping. Guess things didn't turn out so perfect for you either?" I folded my arms across my chest.

He ran his fingers through his hair and then his eyes met mine. "Not everything goes as we plan it, Lib. Sometimes you just have to roll with what life gives you."

My mouth opened and closed. I didn't know what to say. It was the realest thing he'd ever said to me. We were together almost nine months, but never had a real conversation. I never knew his real life goals and dreams, but I did know his favorite drink. Maybe there was something behind the dumb exterior. Or not.

"Hey, Beau. We have another house to hit in Elk Grove. Collect our money and let's go," the other guy yelled from the door, where he was chatting up one of my sorority sisters.

Beth shoved an envelope at him. "You'd better go. Duty calls."

He didn't even look at her as he took the package. "It was good seeing you, Lib. No matter what the circumstances. I always knew you were better than me. Guess this just proves it."

And with that he turned around, leaving me standing there and wondering what the hell just happened.

Chapter 19

After Mom came back to pick me up, I almost passed out in the car. I thought I could sleep the entire next day if no one woke me up.

But then my phone started ringing.

I glanced at the clock beside my bed and saw that it read two AM.

I groaned and hoped it wasn't Beau trying to get in touch with me for some weird, pregnant girl booty call.

But when I saw Blaine's name on my phone, I blew out a sigh of relief, thinking it was just a drunk dial from his bachelor party.

"You know, this is way too early in the morning for phone sex," I said, groggily.

"Meemaw passed away last night," he whispered.

"What?" I sat straight up in bed.

"I didn't want to call you while you were having your party and I knew you'd be sleeping, but I couldn't sleep. I've been lying here just thinking about all of this."

"What happened?"

He sighed. "She was old. She had bad lungs and a bad heart. I don't think they're doing an autopsy. Her nurse went in to check on her after dinner and found her slumped over in her chair."

"Do you want me to come home?"

He sniffled. "I don't want to ask you to do that, but the selfish part of me wants you here. I know you're hormonal and I know we both have a lot of stuff going on, but I need you here. I want you here."

"Okay, Blaine, then I'll be there."

THE NEXT DAY, I TOOK the first flight that I could to New Orleans.

Blaine was waiting for me as soon as I got to baggage claim. He held me in his arms and took in a deep breath as if he was inhaling all of me. "Thanks for coming back."

"Always," I said breathlessly.

I don't know how long we stood there just holding each other. I wasn't going to let go of him and there wasn't any way that he was letting go either. It was until someone bumped into us, possibly not on purpose, that he took my hand and we walked over to the baggage carousel.

My purple suitcase was the only one spinning around and Blaine picked it up, wheeling it with one hand and kept his other hand on mine.

"This couldn't have happened at a worse time," Blaine said as he loaded my suitcase in the back of the car.

"Is there ever a good time for something like this to happen?"

He shrugged and opened my door. "No. But it just sucks that we have a few weeks before our wedding and now we'll be getting ready for a funeral. My Aunt Mary, my dad's sister, is on her way in. My meemaw's brothers and sisters are all gone, so now Dad and Aunt Mary get to stress out together about all of the family finances, plus get ready for our wedding."

I winced. "Do you want to maybe push the wedding back?"

He got in the car and shook his head. "Are you crazy? We've already sent out invitations. Your mom has the tent, table, and chairs rented. Besides, Meemaw would have wanted us to keep going."

"My mom rented the tent and table and chairs?" I raised my eyebrows.

"You didn't know? She wrote my mama a big check. Like a really big one. Mama didn't want to keep it, so your mom just said that she wanted to pay for more things then. I guess that was one of the things they agreed on."

I slowly shook my head. I didn't know whether to be angry or upset or what I wanted to feel. I was so tired. I was tired all the freaking time. All my mom had was money, it was her way of solving every problem. "I didn't know any of that."

"Yeah, Mama felt too proud to take your mama's money, but then she figured it was her baby's wedding too, so I guess they came to an agreement."

Now it made sense why the two were women were so friendly when they were at Lenora's and at the Crabtrees' place. I didn't know what to think of that. Was I mad that my mom even offered? Or was I grateful that she did and just wanted the best wedding for me?

I didn't know what to think, so I just didn't think and let Blaine hold my hand as we headed toward his house.

A small gray car that I didn't recognize was parked in the driveway alongside Alicia and Meg's family cars. Everyone was sitting on the front porch and as soon as we pulled in, Abby raced off the front porch and into Blaine's arms.

"Uncle Blaine, I thought you were never coming back!"

"Aw, of course I came back, Abs."

She stared at him wide-eyed. "You're not going to Heaven like Meemaw?"

He patted her back and set her down. "No, Abby. Not for a long time."

I smiled at her as she danced away. She obviously didn't know what was going on and it had to be hard to explain it to a three-year-old. I was about eight or nine when my grandma died and I really didn't remember much about her other than her being sick. Cancer takes some people in an instant and some people it hangs on to and gives them a slow painful death. All I ever saw was her weak, sitting in a hospital room, never enjoying life. At least Meemaw got to spend her final days at home.

Vicki stepped down the porch steps with another woman beside her. She was a few years younger than Vicki with brown curly hair and dark circles under her eyes with a tear-streaked face. "Libby, this is Blaine's Aunt Mary, Arthur's younger sister," Vicki said.

I put my hand out but Aunt Mary bypassed it and hugged me. "It's so nice to meet you, Libby. I've heard so much about you."

I gently hugged her back. I wished I could have said that I'd heard so much about her, but all I really knew was that Blaine had an aunt that lived in Mississippi and he only really saw her at Christmas. "It's nice to meet you, too."

"My husband and girls will be on their way in tomorrow, then you'll get to meet the whole family."

I nodded. "That'll be great."

I didn't actually mean it. It seemed like the only times families got together was for weddings and funerals. We were only a few weeks from our wedding and now this had to fall on the Crabtree family. I didn't know if a wedding would be the shining light they'd need after this tragedy or if a dark cloud would just hang over it.

Blaine put his arm around my waist. "And the plus side of that is that my cousins Kendall and Chelly will be staying in my room, so I'll be sleeping in yours."

I turned slowly toward Blaine. "In my room?"

Vicki smiled. "Dee said that it would be fine if Blaine stayed with you all while the family was in for a few days. It'll make things easier with everyone coming in for the funeral and it'll give y'all practice for the future."

Blaine couldn't hide his smile. He may have been upset when he called the other night, but I guess he found a silver lining in tragedy.

Now only if we could both fit in my twin-size bed without killing each other.

I'D NEVER ACTUALLY slept in the same bed as a guy.

Weird. I know.

When I dated Beau, I never stayed the night at his fraternity house and since Blaine lived with his parents, and I lived with Aunt Dee, we never really got the chance to share a bed.

I wished I would have bought a cute pair of pajamas at Lenora's or something because my usual over-sized t-shirt and shorts weren't exactly the sexiest thing to wear for my first sleepover.

Blaine emerged from the bathroom in a pair of plaid pajama pants and a plain white t-shirt. I would have rather had him in nothing at all, but given the fact that Aunt Dee wanted us to keep the bedroom door open, I guess he figured being clothed was a better option.

"Ready for bed, Sleeping Beauty?" he asked.

"If I'm Sleeping Beauty, does that make you the beast?" I asked, sliding the covers down and scooting against the wall.

He smiled and slid in next to me, pulling the covers of both of us. I expected the bed to be crowded, but it was more of a feeling of warmth. Like being safe, pressed against him. "I think you just mixed up two different fairy tales."

"No. I just made up my own fairy tale."

He turned off the light and laid his head on the pillow, turning toward me. The moon cast a thin light from the window, illuminating his bright blue eyes. "Yeah? Is the beast a redneck boy from Louisiana and the princess a girl from Chicago?"

I leaned in and gently kissed his lips. "Something like that, except the guy is more of a Southern Casanova."

He laughed. "I like that."

"And I like you."

"Promise?" he asked, putting his hand on my cheek and running his thumb along my jaw line.

"Always," I whispered and kissed his thumb before closing my eyes and letting sleep take over.

MEEMAW'S FUNERAL CAME and went, but Blaine's relatives stayed, something I definitely wasn't expecting.

I guess Meemaw had a lot of finances and things they needed to go over in her will, so Aunt Mary was staying for as long as it took to go through that.

Which meant that Blaine was staying at Aunt Dee's.

We were counting down the days now until the wedding and I still had two out of four of my summer classes to finish. They were quick, three week classes, and all online, but that meant that I was constantly on my laptop doing tests and trying to get all my homework in. And Blaine was left to a lot of the finishing touches on the wedding.

We were sitting on the couch, both with our computers on our laps. I was taking an online quiz and he was going through the guest list. "So, I guess Dad's cousin Lydia can't come in since she used her vacation time for the funeral, so I'm going to move the Sinclairs to the table her and her family were at."

"Uh huh," I said, trying to figure out the difference between a stalactite and stalagmite.

"And then move Jackson's family up another table and put Dina's mama with them."

"Uh huh." One comes up. One goes down.

"Baby, are you even listening to me?"

I turned to Blaine, shaking my head. "What? Of course I'm listening."

"Then what did I just say?"

"You said something about moving tables."

He groaned. "I'm trying to help you out here, but you have to help me, too."

"Can it wait until after I'm done with this quiz? I just have this and my online final is the day after tomorrow, then I'm done."

He put his head back on the couch. "Is this what it's going to be like all the time? You on your computer, me working all day, then we both come home and sit on our own devices? Is our baby going to be born with an iPhone in his hand?"

I scoffed and rolled my eyes. "You're being ridiculous."

He sighed and set his computer on the coffee table. "Baby, I don't want to be one of those couples that just stays stagnant like old pond water. I don't want us to be sitting next to each other and working on our own thing. I want us to be together. Really together."

I shook my head. "It's easier said than done."

He put his hand on mine. "It doesn't have to be. I know things have been crazy and they're just going to keep getting crazier, but the two of us have always had so much passion. It's fueled everything in our relationship and I just want to keep that. Forever."

"Did you think all of that up just now?" I raised an eyebrow.

He groaned and put one arm around me and the other one on the coffee table. "Sometimes you make me poetic. And sleeping next to you every night, but worrying your Aunt Dee will come in if your bed creaks has me horny basically 24/7. I have to recite song lyrics in my head just to think about anything else besides how good your boobs look in all those new tops."

I shoved him gently. "Stop it!"

He leaned in and tickled my sides. "Stop what?"

I squirmed and giggled, falling back on the couch as he crouched over me, his hands sliding up my sides and raising my shirt as he continued tickling.

"Oh my god, Blaine!"

"That's the sound I like to hear!" He laughed.

I never wanted to escape that moment. It was the first time either of us had really laughed in a long time. We could forget about everything else that was going on and just enjoy each other. That is...until I heard a throat-clearing cough.

We parted and I practically jumped across the couch when I turned and saw Aunt Dee standing in the hall. "I didn't mean to intrude."

"No, sorry for disrespecting your home, ma'am. It won't happen again," Blaine said.

Aunt Dee just nodded then looked at me. "Libby, do you have a moment?"

Oh shit. Was I going to be reprimanded? I was twenty, pregnant, and about to be married, yet I was about to be punished because my fiancé was on top of me in the living room.

"Yes." I stood up and followed her back to her bedroom, where she closed the door.

I closed my eyes and let out a breath before opening them, waiting for the blow. I didn't want to fight with her, but it was a few days away from our wedding and a few days before we could move in our new place. We needed our own space. I needed to be able to be with my husband.

But instead of yelling, Aunt Dee opened her closet and pulled out a white sheet that was draped over a hanger. Slowly, she peeled off the sheet and my eyes widened. Aunt Dee's former wedding dress had transformed into a short lace dress with capped sleeves and scalloped edge that framed the crossover neckline. A silk ivory sash cinched around the middle with a full knee-length skirt that gave it just the right amount of pouf. It was perfect.

"Aunt Dee, this is amazing," I said, breathlessly as I wiped the tears out of my eyes.

"Do you really like it? You don't need to lie to me."

I looked up from the dress to her eyes that were just as watery as mine. "It's perfect. Thank you. Not just for the dress, but for everything. For taking me in. For giving me a job. A home. A future."

She didn't say anything, instead she just took me in her arms and we both let our happy tears flow.

Chapter 20

Our wedding day was finally here.

After the whirlwind of planning, our ups and downs, we were finally going to go to bed as a married couple.

Blaine spent the night at Jackson's, so all of the bridesmaids were getting ready at Aunt Dee's. The place was packed with six bridesmaids, Aunt Dee, my mom, and Vicki running around and doing everyone's hair.

"Libby, did you make sure to eat something? I picked up beignets," Mom said for about the hundredth time since her, Beth, and Luxx walked through the door.

"I'm fine, Mom."

"I'll take one of those donut things though, those are damn good," Krisi said, grabbing one as Vicki layered her hair with bobby pins.

Beth scooted in between Mom and me. She had Luxx swaddled against her in some kind of fabric contraption. "Has anyone talked to Aunt Dee about Grandpa and Leslie?"

Mom and I shared a look.

"Um, well, she knows Grandpa is remarried to a much younger woman...you know, half Grandma's age."

Beth raised an eyebrow. "In other words, you didn't tell her that his much younger wife is also knocked up?"

"Well, when you put it that way." I rolled my eyes.

"Maybe there will be too much going on for her to even notice," Mom said.

And as if Leslie knew we were talking about her, a knock came at the door and I saw Grandpa looking in.

Shit.

This was supposed to be my day. Not one that I had to stress about.

Britt opened the door and there stood Leslie in her typical fashion of a black dress with cherries on it and black leather leggings. Her bump was a little less noticeable in all black. Very little.

"There's our beautiful bride!" she said, putting her arms in the air and waltzing over me to embrace me in a big hug.

"Leslie, Clifton, what are you two doing here?" Mom asked.

Grandpa put his hands in his tailored suit jacket. "I thought I should come see Desiree before the ceremony."

Aunt Dee emerged from the bedroom in her rose-colored sundress. "Clifton!" She ran over and embraced him in a hug.

He let go but still squeezed her hand. "Desiree, I don't believe you've met my wife, Leslie."

Aunt Dee turned toward Leslie, her eyes slowly looking over her bump, then back to her face. "It's nice to meet you, Leslie."

"This doesn't have to be awkward," Leslie said and gave Aunt Dee a big hug.

Everyone held their breath for those few seconds until they let go of each other. Aunt Dee smiled and then looked back at Grandpa. "So, how have you been?"

"We've been good. I'm glad to see that you've taken good care of Libby. She seems really happy."

Aunt Dee put her arm around me. "She's really been a joy. It's been a blessing having her here. Now a year later, I get to watch her walk down the aisle and leave."

I took Aunt Dee's hand and squeezed it. "I'll still be here, Aunt Dee. Always. I'll be at work and you know you're not getting out of babysitting duty."

She looked up at me with happy tears in her eyes. "I know, sha. It's just amazing to see how much you blossomed. The little bird who came in here so lost is now spreading her wings and flying. I couldn't be more proud."

Mom put her hand on my shoulder and squeezed it. "Neither can we."

ONE OF THE WORST THINGS about being pregnant is gas. Okay, gas and heartburn.

"Libby! Seriously! What the hell did you eat this morning?" Kristi yelled, kicking my boot with hers from across the limo that was taking us to the church.

"Sorry! I can't help it!"

"Are you going to be up there, saying your vows and all of sudden just let one rip?" Kristi asked.

"Hey, leave gassy alone!" Beth said.

"Oh, gee, thanks for the new nickname." I rolled my eyes.

"Would you prefer skid mark?" Britt asked.

"I hate all of you," I said, but couldn't help the smile on my face.

I was as big as a house, gassy, and had hella heartburn. But somehow I was happy. All of my friends were there with their hair in fancy updos, faces full of make-up and their purple dresses and cowboy boots. They were all there for me.

"I can't believe this is all happening. I'm really getting married and you're really all here for me," I said, sniffling. The happy tears were falling down my face before I could stop them.

Beth thrusted a tissue at me. "Now, don't cry yet. We have to keep that makeup job straight for pictures. I didn't spend the last forty-five minutes putting all that on you."

"Sorry, baby hormones," I sniffed.

"It's okay, we all get them," Kristi said.

"Even you?" I asked, raising an eyebrow.

She bit down on her bottom lip. "I didn't want to tell you and ruin your big day, but the latest round of shots worked. Little man Crabtree is going to have another best friend in Chicago."

I threw myself across the limo, feeling it shake underneath me, but I didn't care. I embraced Kristi in the biggest hug I could. "Kristi! This is great news! You didn't need to wait to tell me."

She shrugged as I sat down beside her and Dina scooted over so my big pregnant butt could fit in the seat. "I didn't want to try and take your spotlight."

I shook my head. "I don't see it that way at all."

She smiled. "That's why you're the best. You always think of others, no matter what. I wasn't sure how your pregnancy hormones would be either, so I didn't want to push it. I know just in these few short weeks I've become a raging bitch."

"Wait until both of your third trimesters," Beth said.

"Not much longer for mine," I grumbled.

"Hey, it could be worse. You could be stuck working on your feet all day in the Louisiana heat...wait," Dina said and then laughed.

"Hey, at least the shop is air conditioned and I'm sure the boss won't mind if I put my feet up," I said.

Britt laughed. "We'll see if Grandma lets you get away with that one."

I shrugged. "Hey, it couldn't hurt to try. I've gotten away with a lot more."

I'D NEVER BEEN ONE of those girls that dreamed of their wedding day or thought I'd get emotional, but when 'Canon in D' started playing and the church doors opened to see all of my family in friends standing there, the tears openly streaked my cheeks. I had a feeling Beth was silently cursing that I was ruining my makeup.

But I didn't care.

At the end of the aisle, my dad hugged me and whispered in my ear, "I'm proud of you, Libby," then he kissed my cheek, shook Blaine's hand and stepped back.

I looped my arm in Blaine's and turned toward the priest, listening as he spoke the words to us. To our family. To joining of all of us.

I found myself constantly looking over at Blaine and every time I did, he would smile and squeeze my hand. We were finally here. There was no running for either of us.

When he held my hand and said "I do," a new fresh set of tears sprung. Tears of pure joy.

This was real. He was mine and I was his. Forever. For always.

After the service had ended and we took a million pictures, we all drove back to Blaine's parents' house where a large, white tent was set up with dozens of tables all under twinkling lights. A long table sat near the house, with the church ladies behind it. They set up trays of different Louisiana dishes and a large cake with a blonde bride and groom on top.

Before dinner was served, Blaine and I and the bridal party sat at the head table and Beth stood up to give her speech.

She smoothed out her purple shift dress and looked at me, smiling. "As you all know, Libby Gentry is my little sister. Just like Blaine is now, she's been stuck with me for better or for worse."

Everyone laughed at that one.

Then she put her hand on my shoulder and squeezed it. "My little sister has always looked up to me and I haven't always been the best big sister. She lost her way and I had no idea where to point her, so she came here, to Elsbury, and I think if there was a trail for everyone that would point them in the right direction, then this was it for her."

She looked over at Blaine, brushing a tear from her cheek. "Blaine, you've brought out the very best and the worst parts of my sister. But you've been her savior. You've blessed me with my future nephew and now I have the brother that I wanted Libby to be. Keep her on her trail, Blaine. Keep her and my nephew happy like I know you've made her and I promise you she'll do the same."

Blaine nodded and raised his glass as the rest of the bridal party did in a toast.

"Now, I do have one more thing to say, or well...try to say..." Blaine stood up and Beth handed him the microphone.

I raised an eyebrow, looking up at him. We didn't talk about him doing any sort of speech and Blaine wasn't much for public speeches.

"A lot of you have thought we were crazy. Hell, I've thought we were crazy half the time for doing this, but sometimes when you love someone, you're willing to go a little out there for them."

He signaled to Jackson, who nodded and went behind the tent.

"Now, I'm not much of a talker, but I do have a lot that I want to say, so..."

Jackson emerged from behind the tent with Blaine's acoustic guitar in his hand.

"Thank you, Jackson." Blaine nodded and took the guitar, slinging the strap over his shoulder and strumming a few chords.

"As I was saying...they called us crazy when we started out..."

He strummed a few more chords then started singing "Said twenty is too young to know what love's about."

Jackson cupped his hands together "And they'll be together another fifty years."

Blaine laughed, strumming the chords and singing "That's crazy."

He sang the next couple of lines and then all of his groomsmen joined in as he got to the chorus, where I finally realized that he was singing Lee Brice's "Love like crazy".

I watched in awe as his fingers moved along the strings and he sang with a huge smile on his face, the rest of the bridal party joining.

I didn't know the words, but I clapped along and watched.

When Blaine got to the end of the song, he sat down, his blue eyes locked on me. The rest of the bridal party stopped singing and it was if there was no one else in the room but Blaine and me.

"They called us crazy when we started out," he sang.

"And we'll be together another fifty-eight years, if not more, ain't that crazy?"

I shook my head and leaned in and kissed him, which caused an eruption of applause from the crowd.

"Crazy and wonderful," I whispered into his lips as I broke the kiss, keeping my hands on his cheeks.

"Happy one hour anniversary, baby."

I laughed. "Happy one hour anniversary."

AFTER THE LARGE BUFFET was served, the DJ called us out to the wooden dance floor in the middle of the room and a Rascall Flatts song played. It was the song we danced to on the beach at Kristi's wedding and the first song I heard in the car when I followed him back to Aunt Dee's the night we met. The night I had no idea what I was in for.

Blaine pressed his forehead to mine. "We did it. We're really married."

"Did you think we wouldn't be?"

He squeezed my sides. "I think I've known since the minute I saw you that there was no way I wanted to be with anyone else ever again."

"How could you know that?"

He shrugged. "Sometimes you just know. It's this immediate connection. A spark. It was the thing that made me jump up and talk to you. The thing that keeps me looking at you every single day and wonder how the hell a beautiful girl like you could be with a guy like me."

"I could say the same thing about you."

He pulled me closer, his hands resting on the small of my back. "Well, for better or for worse, it's you and me. I know things might not always be perfect, but I'm going to try and be the best damn husband and father I can be."

I leaned and lightly kissed his lips. "You already are."

"Um, Libby?"

I felt Sawyer's nimble fingers on my shoulder before I turned to see him. I convinced Blaine to make him a groomsman since I had so many bridesmaids and he had an extra space. That said, Sawyer wasn't the best at pulling off the rugged look in jeans and a blazer, so he rebelled and wore his skinny jeans and suspenders.

"I hate to interrupt your dance, but you know your favorite blonde? She may or may not be in the middle of a fight with your fiery redhead bridesmaid."

My eyes widened and I went to move, but Blaine was quicker, letting go of me and barreling off the dance floor toward the corner of the tent.

Of course Nikki would find a way to ruin something at my wedding. And of course, Blaine would go after her.

Kristi was standing under the weeping willow with her hands on her hips and Nikki was directly across from her, swaying a bit. Even though she was in a pale blue one-shoulder dress and heels, she still looked like she was ready for a fight. Always the redneck princess.

"What the hell is going on?" Blaine asked, pushing his way between the two of them.

Kristi shook her head. "Ask your little tawdry friend who seems to think draining half a bottle and then crying about how much she loves you is a good idea."

"Nikki..." Blaine stared at her like he was reprimanding a toddler.

Nikki rolled her eyes. "Oh, please, like you're going to be happy with Libby. Like, really, who believes that?"

Blaine put his hands out and stepped forward. "Now, I think you've had a little too much to drink. Why don't I go find Bubba to take you home?"

She swatted his hands. "No! I'm speaking the truth! Do you really think you're going to be happy? You're just marrying her because she's knocked up and now you have to go home to her bitching every night. You'll never get to go out with your friends. This is the end of the line, Blaine Crabtree and I hope you're happy with it."

Kristi turned to me. "Can I just punch her now?"

I shook my head before stepping forward, pushing Blaine out of the way. "Look here, Nicole Sinclair, I didn't want to invite you to this wedding, hell, I didn't want you anywhere in my life. I don't care that we did a little kiss and makeup at Cotillion, you're still a pain in my ass. I'm not saying I'm sorry that Blaine loves me and that we're together, what I am sorry for is the fact that you can't seem to get past that. For that, I'm sorry that you're stuck with your miserable self forever."

Nikki opened her mouth to speak, but Blaine stepped in between us. "I think that's enough, you two. Nikki, I'll get Bubba. Libby, meet me back on the dance floor in five."

I raised my eyebrows. "Think you can tell me what to do?"

He leaned in, smiling before he pulled me close and placed a huge kiss on my lips. "I think I just might try, wifey."

I nodded behind him. "Think she's going to be a problem?"

He put his hands on either side of my face. "You mean, do you think I'm worried or taking to heart what she said? Absolutely not. I took those vows today and I meant them. We're going to have some crazy ups and downs, maybe even more than we've already had, but a few words from a jealous ex ain't gonna affect me."

I smiled and leaned in for another kiss. "Good."

BLAINE TURNED OUT OF the long driveway and down the street.

This was it. We were married.

Okay, technically we'd been married since we got the marriage license at the courthouse the day before, but now we'd said our vows. We'd had our first dance as a couple and been sent off with our friends and family holding sparklers.

Now we had the rest of our lives together and the car was packed with enough stuff to spend our first night in our new place.

At least, I thought we were.

Instead of going toward the highway, Blaine turned in the other direction.

I arched an eyebrow. "I know you've lived here a lot longer than me, but I'm pretty sure it's the other direction to New Orleans."

A ghost of a smile danced on his lips but he didn't look at me. "We aren't going to New Orleans."

"Then where are we going?"

He put his hand on mine and squeezed it. "It's a surprise."

I normally would have whined and protested for him to tell me. But after having the best day of my life and with his thumb rubbing over the bridge of my knuckles, I just smiled and let him surprise me.

He turned down a gravel side road that I'd never been on before. It was lined with a forest of willows with branches that barely missed sweeping the top of the car.

Blaine put on his turn signal and turned left. The only thing lighting the path were Blaine's headlights, so I couldn't see anything more than the gravel path ahead of us.

That is, until a small open air porch greeted us. It was attached to a Southern-style white home with large windows and plantation shutters.

There were a few bed and breakfasts in the Elsbury area. When the economy took a downturn, a lot of people opened their older homes to guests that wanted to stay outside of the hustle and bustle of the city. I figured that's what this was.

Blaine turned off the engine and got out of the car, coming around the passenger door to help me out.

"Well, this is cute," I said as Blaine led me down the path to the front porch.

"I think it could use some landscaping. Maybe plant some flowers magnolias upfront. Pave the path and driveway."

I arched an eyebrow. This wasn't like Blaine to start critiquing places we went to. But he was also smiling, so I didn't want to ruin his mood.

We stepped on the porch with its green wooden floor and a small porch swing barely moved in the still night air.

Blaine pulled his keys out of his pocket and searched through them until he pulled out a gold one and slid it in the door, then pushed it open.

Before I could ask why he had a key to the place, he swooped me up in his arms, fireman style, and carried me over the threshold before setting me down in the foyer and turning on the lights.

"Blaine, what is all of this?"

He stepped in front of me and took my hands. "This is our home."

"What?" I widened my eyes.

He let go of one of my hands and led me through the foyer and past two darkened rooms and then turned on a light to a room with green floral wallpaper and a large stone fireplace. "This was my meemaw's. I was going to wait to move in, but tonight before the reception, Dad and Aunt Mary gave me the keys. They said it was always supposed to be mine and Meemaw would want us to move in right away and for this to be the place we bring our son home to."

Tears welled up in my eyes as I looked over the dark wood floors and the crown molding.

Blaine stepped closer. "Now, I know it needs some work, but I can do that. Dad will help me and we can make it our own."

I shook my head, a single tear falling down my cheek.

Blaine brushed the tear away with his thumb. "Aw, baby, don't tell me that you hate it."

I shook my head and kissed him deeply, letting my lips say what I couldn't.

This all started with a piece of paper saying I'd failed out of college. Now we had a piece of paper saying we were married. Those pieces all began a paper trail for the rest of our life together and it was going to start and end in our new home.

If you enjoyed this book, please leave a review on
GoodReads or whatever online retailer you picked up
this book from.
It keeps the author happy and you get your own chance to
be a writer :)

About the Author

Magan Vernon has been living off of reader tears since she wrote her first short story in 2004. She now spends her time killing off fictional characters, pretending to plot while she really just watches Netflix, and she tries to do this all while her two young children run amuck around her Texas ranch.

Sign up for her newsletter[1]

Or follow her Social Media

Facebook[2]

Twitter[3]

GoodReads[4]

Pinterest[5]

Blog[6]

---

1. http://eepurl.com/qIJA5

2. http://www.facebook.com/pages/Author-Magan-Vernon/215620155165079

3. https://twitter.com/MaganVernon

4. http://www.goodreads.com/author/show/5237606.Magan_Vernon

5. http://pinterest.com/authormagan/

6. http://www.thepunchingbagfightsback.blogspot.com/

Acknowledgements

Over 200,000 words and that many copies sold of the first two books in this series. From the bottom of my heart I have to thank everyone who picked up this book and gave me a chance whether they hated it or loved it.

A big shot out goes to my betas Lheanne Spicer, Ellie So, and Kelly Viel. Thank you for helping me to make this book one of the best of the series.

My PA, Alissa Glenn, without you I don't think I'd be able to get anything done. EVER. You're the paper to my wings. The one who makes me fly.

My mother-in-law and father-in-law, thank you for taking care of the kids so I could finish these stories.

My husband, Timothy Ray, thanks for being the southern gentleman that inspired my Blaine.

Brandon Lane, thank you for being the perfect cover model. I didn't know there was a real Blaine out there until I saw you. You've been so helpful with everything!

Michael Meadows, you're my favorite. Don't tell my husband. You found me my Blaine. You found a place that looked like a bayou in Arizona! You're amazing!

Donna Dull, my cover designer. Thanks for putting up with my crazy demands!

Kellie Montgomery, I don't know how many aints there were, but I'm glad you don't hate me for them.

There are so many people that have helped this serious come into fruition and I feel like I'm forgetting so many, but know that I paper heart every single one of you!